love among the shamrocks collection

the next generation

Book Two

The Song of Heart's Desire

M. KATHERINE CLARK

Other works by

M. Katherine Clark

The Greene and Shields Files
       Blood is Thicker Than Water
       Once Upon a Midnight Dreary
       Old Sins Cast Long Shadows
       Tales from the Heart, Novelettes

Love Among the Shamrocks Collection
       Under the Irish Sky
       Across the Irish Sea
       On the River Shannon
       The Land Across the Sea, an Emmet O'Quinn Short

Love Among the Shamrocks Collection the Next Generation
       In Dublin Fair City
       Song of Heart's Desire
       Chasing After Moonbeams – Coming 2021

The Wolf's Bane Saga
       Wolf's Bane
       Lonely Moon
       Midnight Sky
       Star Crossed
       Moon Rise
       Moon Song, a Companion Guide

Dragon Fire
       Heart of Fire
       Will of Fire – Coming 2021

Soundless Silence, *a Sherlock Holmes Novel*

The Rest is Silence, *an Edmond Holmes Novel* – Coming 2021

Silent Whispers, *a Scottish Ghost Story*

Silent Night, *a Scottish Christmas Ghost Story* – Coming Soon

To all those who have lost and never let it get them down. Those who picked up the broken pieces and made something even more beautiful!

Prologue

Saying goodbye to someone you've known and loved for over a decade was one thing. But saying goodbye to a life cut short and one you never got a chance to see? That was something entirely different.

As Lachlan O'Quinn stared down at the freshly dug grave and the casket containing his wife and stillborn daughter being lowered into the open earth, he felt the last thread of his will to live, cut clean. The smell of petrichor, fresh earth before the rain, burned his nostrils and the tears he had shed, refused to stop. They had tried so long to have a child. He and his Karin. It wasn't fair he never even got the chance to see his beautiful daughter's eyes.

Unsure if he would ever be able to forgive the teenager who had caused the car accident simply to answer a text on his phone, Lachlan kept his eyes down, focused on the grave and his anger hidden from his family who surrounded him.

But as soon as the music started, he wasn't sure he would survive. All the emotions raged within him and nothing could stop it. Falling to his knees as his muscles gave out, he reached toward the shimmering brown casket that held his heart and soul. As it was being lowered, he hoped the earth would swallow him up and he could be with his two favorite people in the world. The ground was coming closer and though tears rained down his cheeks, he didn't care. The pain was too much. He felt as if someone was cutting his chest open and scooping out his heart with a teaspoon.

Just as he thought he would get his wish, a strong hand landed on his shoulder and pulled him back. Someone screamed but only after the sound echoed, did he realize it was him. His father's arms came around him as Cabhan knelt beside him. He held him close but even a father's love and support could not end the heartache. Lachlan wept into his father's shoulder as the first of the dirt was tossed into the grave.

Cabhan pulled back and stared into his son's eyes, the same toffee color mirrored his pain. But his father wouldn't understand, he couldn't understand. He never lost his wife or a child. They all stood near him that morning. But as much as his father tried to help, nothing would be able to block out the pain of seeing his wife lying on the emergency C-section table, face bloody, eyes closed, and hearing no cry from their child as she was ripped from her mother's body. Nothing could stop it. Nothing but death and he welcomed it. Wished for it. Hoped it would swallow him up just as the earth was swallowing the only good thing to ever happen to him.

Chapter One

Ten years later

Dr. Lachlan O'Quinn looked around the mostly empty office of his veterinarian practice in Dublin, Ireland. The last nine years in the small, but booming practice were some of the hardest of his life. But seeing it empty, tugged at memories of emotions he no longer claimed to have. Turning when his secretary sighed loudly beside him, he took in his cousin's profile. Egan McArdle turned to him.

"Are you sure about this, Lach?" He asked. Being a cousin on his mother's side, Lachlan turned a deaf ear when he called him by the family nickname when they were alone. That, and he owed his cousin a lot over the years.

After his wife Karin died, Lachlan lacked purpose and drive to do anything. Egan negotiated a lease on a set of small offices on the outskirts of Dublin and nearly forced his signature on the document. Since moving from Kerry to Dublin town, Lachlan successfully buried the worst of the pain and continued living... though *living* was too strong a word for the half-life he maintained. Stashing away his emotions made him much more methodical and, in some cases, more like a machine than a human. Lachlan lived every day waiting for the morning he could rejoin his wife.

Still, the idea of moving back home, stirred his heart more than he was willing to admit.

"I'm sure," he stated. "Da's retiring and there's no one to take over. I'm the logical one"

"Logical," Egan shook his head and sighed again, placing his hands on his slim hips. "All right, Spock. What else needs to be done?"

"Everything in the moving van?" Lachlan asked.

"Yep," he answered. "Perfectly packed as per your instructions."

"Good," Lachlan nodded. "How about the flat?"

"That team, led by your brother, is already on their way to Killarney. He wanted you to head over before you left and check it out. Also, give final keys."

Lachlan dug in his pocket. Offering Egan the keys to his flat, he locked eyes with him.

"I'd rather not go back," he said. "It's hard enough leaving here."

Egan nodded and took the keys.

With one more look around, he refused to feel the stirrings of sadness in his chest. Nearly ten years, the office on Grange Road near the National Park, was his home away from home. The one good thing about his solitude, was the ability to meet his cousins Trevor or Egan for lunch or sometimes supper when Trevor was studying at Trinity University. But since he graduated five years ago and moved with his wife to America, they hadn't stayed as close as before which saddened him… if he could *feel* sad.

Having Trevor and his other family, his Uncle Innis' family, less than twenty minutes away was a lifeline to his self-preservation and prevented him from ending at all. Too many times he had come in early, gone straight to the tranquilizers, grabbed a syringe, and nearly ended his life, but the thought of his family stopped him and once, his Uncle Innis had walked in, just as Lachlan held the syringe to his skin. The shock then look of determination reflected in his uncle's eyes haunted Lachlan. Since then, Innis had made sure to call him and set him up with a counselor. Talking about the loss had helped him put the desire of self-harm away but it never fully left the back of his mind. The only thing that helped him, was work. Animals never let him down and they never got too close to his heart.

"Lach, I'm gonna ask you one more time. Are you sure about this?" Egan questioned. "Because it's not too late. You can tell Dr. Harris you aren't moving out."

"The lease is already switched," he shook his head. "Besides, I couldn't do that to my da' or my brother."

His baby brother was thirteen years younger. At twenty-five, Oisín had started his own moving company and it was quite the hit with the ladies of all ages because the movers had to be buff young men, willing to wear nothing but a kilt and boots, a remnant of when he had studied in Scotland.

Not caring what the old biddies, or young women in his complex thought about the men moving his things, Lachlan only wanted to help his brother's business but refused to be in the same location as the *Rough and Buff* movers. There was a lot he'd do for his little brother but seeing him and his college buddies shirtless and in a kilt was not one of them.

"I'm driving straight through tonight," Lachlan stated. "I should be there directly after them, so I'll go to the office first. They know to set that up before the cottage, right?"

"It's in the notes," Egan replied. "Whether or not they read is another issue."

Lachlan gave him his usual blank look. His cousin may have been only thirty-two, but he was as ornery and cantankerous about the younger generation as any seventy-year-old.

"Well, since there's no convincing you otherwise, I'll just say I'm going to miss you, ya old goat," he said.

"Don't start that," Lachlan replied. He was already feeling the creeping fingers of sadness tickle his belly and, as with any emotion, he pushed it firmly away.

Egan cleared his throat and looked away. "Still, you're family."

"Kerry is four hours away."

"Aye, but who do I call now when I want a pint and don't want to drink alone?"

Lachlan allowed the corner of his mouth to tick up.

"Well, there is this novel idea of getting friends."

"Ah, friends are overrated," he waved him off. Lachlan scoffed, the closest thing to a chuckle he'd done in a decade. If he was going to be perfectly frank, he was going to miss him too.

Clearing his own throat, he offered a goodbye embrace. They clung to each other and thumped the other's back.

"I'm gonna miss you," Lachlan said, surprised by the emotion welling in his chest. Egan had been there. He had been there when Lachlan worked himself nearly to death. He had been there when Lachlan drank himself into an oblivion on the five year anniversary and he had been there when Lachlan cut off all emotion and still, he teased him, was there for him, helped him see he had reason for still being on earth and now he was leaving that all behind.

He tightened his embrace on his cousin and then let him go. Holding a hand to his shoulder, he stood arm's length away from him. Only then did he realize, for all his fluff and fuddle, Egan McArdle was his best friend. Or as close to a best friend as he allowed himself to have.

A breath in, as deep as he had ever been able to take since his wife died, he squeezed his cousin's shoulder and nodded to him.

"Ah, get on the road," Egan huffed. "Call me if you get tired."

"I will," Lachlan promised. "Thank you again. For everything."

"You're welcome," Egan said. "Tell your mom, my auntie, I love her when you see her."

Lachlan promised he would and, not wanting to draw out their goodbye any longer, he grabbed his medical bag, personal duffel bag, he knew he would be living out of until he could unpack, and took his car keys. One final look around the office, he let Egan out, and shut and locked the door.

Not one for hyperbole, but it felt as if he was shutting the door on his life the last few years. He had started there as a new vet nine years ago, not wanting to stay in Kerry. He had left with no plan, barely any money, and a hole in his chest where his heart used to be. Traveling to Dublin on the last tank of gas he could afford and a picnic lunch his mother had packed for him, he had nowhere to go. Fortunately, his Uncle Innis, his father's brother had taken him in but there was only so long he could stay there with all his younger cousins.

Egan helped him find a place and though it wasn't far from his family the silence was golden and on some particularly bad days it was deafening.

He had done what he could to survive, not because he wanted to, but because his self-preservation prevented him from taking his own life, always reminding him of his wife's final words to him.

"You know how much I love you and how I can always rely on you to see the future where I can't."

Of course, she had said them teasingly after he had told her, after their first child was born, he saw about five more and a cottage in the countryside overlooking the Atlantic Ocean.

That never happened, of course and he left Kerry. He hadn't been back in years. He hadn't seen Karin's name on the headstone. He couldn't. That made him weak, but he didn't care.

As he sat in Dublin rush hour traffic, his gaze was pulled to the piece of metal wrapped around his finger. The sun glinted off the gold as it played peekaboo with the clouds.

He never thought he would be a widower at only twenty-eight, but he was. Now at thirty-eight, he had devoted his life to taking care of animals and the only human interactions he had, was the worried owners who wanted to make sure he was the best, which he was. Or the occasional pint he would have with one or other of his family members.

All other times, he was alone.

All because some stupid kid thought answering a text was more important than keeping his eyes on the road. *He* walked away, but his wife never walked anywhere again. The usual pain that came with the memories welled as he stared at the wedding band. He hadn't taken it off. He never would. Karin was everything to him. He loved her since they were sixteen, married her at eighteen and never saw her again at twenty-eight.

Someone honked and he looked up, the cars in front of him had moved and he was holding up the line. With a wave to the car behind him, he pulled forward.

Breaking through the heavy traffic, he was finally on the road, going home with all the memories that came with it, but starting his life over.

Chapter Two

Corinne McDonnagh stared at her father in disbelief. "You did what?" She demanded.

Her father looked down and twisted his fingers, a telltale sign he wasn't teasing.

"I'm so sorry, love," he was serious. "I didn't... He tricked me. Made me not know what I was saying."

"No, dad, that was the *Johnny Walker*. How could you?" She demanded. "The house, the car, hell, even your business, I understand but... me?"

Again, he looked away. His stocky five-foot seven-inch

frame shuddered.

"He's always wanted you," he shrugged.

"And that gives you the right to gamble me away?" Her voice took on a shrill tone.

Callum McDonnagh had a problem. A problem with cards and drink. It had already cost more than Corinne was willing to forgive but his latest was over the line.

"You gambled me, and you lost," she summarized. "So now, you expect me to roll over and allow that... That..."

How do you describe the heir of the mob in London? Anthony Rossi, the son of Ricardo Rossi, the known Italian mobster, was a slick haired, porn 'stache, smarmy thirty year old, who sported aviator sunglasses even at night, and a suit that cost more than a year's worth of her wages as a vet tech. She'd seen him, once, at a not for profit gala for the Humane Society where she volunteered. The Rossi's were the greatest donor.

Humane. Yeah right.

She suppressed a shudder when she remembered his golden eyed gaze from across the room. He had sauntered over to her as she stood beside the board chairman and asked why *she* wasn't on the silent auction roster. The chairman gave a nervous chuckle but did nothing to defend her. That was the story of her life when it came to men. Her father, her ex-boyfriend, her primary school friend, they all let her down and never defended her. There was only one man who took care to always be there, and she stopped a smile when she remembered him swooping in, wrapping an arm around her waist, and reminding her she owed him a dance.

Geoffrey Ainsley had always been there for her. If only they were attracted to each other and he wasn't such a great friend, they would have been married by then.

Her focus back on her father, she stared at his pleading eyes. Was that the look he always gave her mother after losing everything? Was that why her body finally gave out and she died? Corinne hardened her features as every time she thought of her mother, tears pricked her eyes.

"I'm so sorry, Corrie," he said. "But he'll kill me."

"And what about me?" she demanded.

"It's only a trial marriage. You be out of it in five years," he tried to make it sound like five years was nothing. And honestly, at twenty-eight, five years wouldn't be horrible but five years with him? Never. She'd be dead before that and she be damned if she didn't fight.

She shook her head. Her father's face fell. "You condemn me to death."

"You condemned me to a fate worse than death."

"Corrie—"

"No, no, it's over, Dad. I've forgiven a lot of things as you well know, but this is beyond anything I can forgive. How could you?" She held up a hand when he opened his mouth to speak. "No, no, on second thought, don't answer that. There's nothing you could say to make this remotely better." She grabbed her purse and phone.

"Where are you going?" he questioned.

"It's better you don't know. Wouldn't want you to gamble that away, too. Don't contact me. Don't try to find me."

"Corrie!"

She slammed the door as she left.

Chapter Three

Lachlan ran his hand across Donovan's flank and down his chestnut leg. The horse whinnied and pawed deep gashes in the dirt.

"What seems to be the problem?" Lachlan asked Old Widow McKeel who stood at the entrance of the horse barn.

"Problem?" she questioned.

"With Donovan," he said indicating the horse.

"Oh, well, he's just not himself," she replied.

Lachlan suppressed his groan. Since arriving back in Kerry

County, he had been called out nearly every week to multiple farms and had many visits to his father's – *his* office – and all were the same reasoning. But what was annoying was, they were all widowed women, or those who had single daughters or granddaughters who conveniently showed up while he was there and invited to tea simply to be set up with him.

Sure enough, he turned to look at her, her eyes were glued to his arse.

The woman was older but did not deserve the nickname of *Old Widow McKeel*. She was a blushing young bride forty years ago when, at twenty-two, she married Farmer McKeel, a man twice widowed but the wealthiest farmer in the county. When McKeel died, she became the most notorious widow. A *wealthy cougar* was the most talked about and apparently, she set her sights on Lachlan… or rather, his arse.

"Well," he gently patted the horse's side. "Looks like he's all right now, so he is. If something else happens, give me a call." He gathered his things.

"It's not just the horse," she stepped forward. He froze. "I've been feeling poorly too."

What was this a cheap movie? Where are the cameras? He thought. "Sorry to hear that. Doc Needlers just moved in down the street. I'll send him over."

Standing, he nodded in her direction and walked sternly to the barn door.

"Don't you want to help me?" Her voice came out sounding husky. Lachlan sighed.

It had happened before. Not with her, but others. He'd been told he was attractive. He took after his father in certain lights and the O'Quinn lads were known throughout Kerry to be handsome. Along with the grey at his temples and throughout his natural brown hair, terms like *Silver Fox* had been thrown around.

Did he miss sex? Well, he was a red-blooded male. But what he missed more than that was the connection that grew over time. Random hookups or one night stands were not his thing.

"Mrs. McKeel," he began. "Thank you, but I'm not interested. If you are truly feeling poorly, I highly suggest going to see Doc Needlers."

He turned and promptly closed his eyes. The crazy woman had pulled her top off and the lace bra did little to cover her breasts.

"Please, put your clothes back on," he muttered. "I will send you my bill." There would be no bill, but he had to think of something to say.

"You don't want to make an enemy of me, O'Quinn," she called after him.

"I'll take my chances," he replied.

"I told you to give up your v-card to that one guy in University. That way you wouldn't have to worry about this," Geoffrey Ainsley said as he poured wine into his chic stemless glasses.

"I'm not giving *it* up for no reason," Corinne replied, tucking her left leg under her as she sat on his couch.

"And a hot guy isn't a valid reason?" He questioned, handing her the glass, and sitting beside her.

"Some of us aren't sluts," she answered, taking a large sip.

"Oh, harsh," he winced, teasingly. "But accurate." Corinne

breathed a laugh. "I can't help it if I love my women."

"Mmhmm," she grinned. "Only women?" He gave her a sardonic look but didn't respond to her insinuation.

"You know I offered to… help you out with that little issue." He winked.

"And you and I agreed, we didn't want to ruin our friendship."

"Yeah, yeah," he replied. "Pity that."

"Besides, I don't think the estimable Lady Winifred Russell would appreciate it."

"Low blow, love," Geoff replied. "You know we don't even like each other."

"You could try, you know. She will be the future Lady Garvey, Mrs. Geoffrey Ainsley."

"Do I need reminding?" He questioned and took a large sip. "Ugh, this isn't strong enough for that conversation." He motioned to the wine.

"I still don't understand, if you really don't want to agree to the betrothal, why don't you tell your father no."

"Have you tried saying no to the Earl of Torrington?"

"No, but if you don't love her…"

"Aristocratic marriages have nothing to do with love. An heir and a spare, and then we will be able to do our own thing. She's had lovers in the past I'm sure. She can have any she wants after my sons are born. So long as we're both discrete nothing should prevent us from living quite different lives. The only time we will need to see each other is when we have public events to attend."

"Have you talked to her about it?"

"Nope," he shook his head. "But it is the twenty-first century. So long as for the first two years or however long it takes to have two sons, she is loyal to me, I will be loyal to her. It's all very romantic."

"I'm sure," Corinne rolled her eyes. "Arranged marriages… what a pair we are."

"Hey, at least you'll be out of yours in five years," he teased.

"I'm serious, Geoff," she said, her voice catching.

"I know you are, sweetheart. I'm sorry. This isn't good. I'm just trying to make you laugh," he stated.

"I know, but I'm scared, Geoff. This is tantamount to prostitution and rape." She shook.

"It'll be all right. You stay here tonight or for however long you want," he placed an arm around her shoulders. She leaned her head against him.

"Thank you," she answered. "But I don't want you drawn into this. My father screwed up… again but this time it's unforgivable. I don't even think money will dissuade Rossi… not that I have any."

"You know I'd help," Geoff offered. "I'm not exactly Vanderbilt but I have some money. I'll even go talk to my father."

She looked up at him, "You'd do that for me?"

"Absolutely, I would do anything for you, love. Surely you know that by now."

Geoff's father, the renowned pacifist and tenth Duke of Torrington disowned his son when he enlisted in the latest war with the Middle East. Since Geoffrey's subsequent heroic career ended in an honorable medical discharge from Her Majesty's Army, Special Reconnaissance Division, his playboy and *laissez faire* attitude caused him to be in the news in various lights sparking controversary, questions of his sexuality, and causing scandals to wreck the name of Ainsley, all of which, his father detested.

Since he was an only child, he could not be disinherited, but his father had cut off his allowance. The duke tolerated Geoff for his mother's sake. But they were hardly friends.

"Thank you," she said. "But I would never want to force you to do that. I know how it would make you feel."

"You aren't forcing. I'm offering. He has connections," Geoff offered. "I'll at least talk to him."

Corinne nodded and kissed his cheek. They were silent for a long while just watching the flames on the gas fireplace jump and drinking their wine.

"I need to get away," she finally said. "Somewhere they won't find me."

"Like where?"

"I don't know, but if I'm not in London, maybe he won't come for me."

"You know Peter lives in America with his fiancée, but he has family in Ireland."

"Peter?" she questioned. Geoff nodded. "You still keep in contact with him?"

"Of course, he's my best friend."

"I thought I was your best friend," she pouted teasingly.

"You're my best girl friend," he winked.

"You and he met in Afghanistan, right?"

"Yep," he took another sip of wine. "We were sent to find him. He had gotten himself captured. That was the beginning of our friendship. They're coming to stay with me when they travel to Europe for their honeymoon."

"Awe, that's generous of you," she replied.

"We were always friends," he justified. "And I'm glad he's found someone to love. Vivian's a nice girl… for an American."

She laughed at his quintessential English arrogance. "Isn't Peter American, too?" she questioned.

"All I'm saying is maybe try Ireland," he changed the subject. "It's beautiful. And desolate and separated by a sea. It could be perfect."

"I can't say I've ever been," she calculated the money in her savings. "Do you know how much it would be?"

"Don't worry about that," he answered. "I'll take care of it."

At that moment, Oscar, Corinne's Irish wolfhound padded over to her from the bed she set up in the guest room. He whined but knew Geoff's house rule. *No dog on the couch.*

She stroked her dog's head and scratched behind the ears. "I can't ask that of you," she said. "I'll find a way. I have always wanted to go see mum's homeland."

"Let's go tomorrow and open a joint account, my name as primary and that way I can put some money in there for you. I can also help by paying your bills while you're away."

"That's too much for you to do."

"Would you stop? It's not. Not for my girl," he answered, refilling her wine glass. "And besides, you have what? *Two* bills."

She conceded. "Okay, I would say no if I had a choice."

"I know you would. But that's what friends are for."

"I love you, Geoff."

"Love you too," he winked and clinked his glass to hers. "It'll be okay. I won't let anything happen to you."

Corinne took a sip and a deep breath. She rested her head on his shoulder, feeling his arm come around her, and stared into the fireplace. Her body, mind, and heart heavy with thoughts and fear. Hopefully, if she closed her eyes, she could wish everything back to normal.

Chapter Four

Lachlan drummed his fingers on the desk. There was only so long he could sit there with nothing to do. Checking his calendar, he shook his head. Nothing. Huffing a sigh, he stood. Enough was enough. He needed to work. He needed patients. *Where is everyone?*

Opening the door, he startled his secretary, who jumped and looked over at him.

"Dr. O'Quinn?" She questioned. "Is everything all right?"

"No, Donna, it's not. Where is everyone?"

"Everyone, sir?" She questioned.

"All the patients? I was run off my feet for the last three months and now..." he gestured to the empty waiting room. "Where is everyone?"

Her eyes grew wide. "Well... ehm..." She knew something, it was written all over her face.

She had been his father's secretary for over forty years and the town's gossip almost as bad as his own Grandma Deirdre. Almost.

"Come into my office," he turned back and waited at the door. Tentatively, she walked in. As soon as she cleared the threshold, he shut the door. Crossing his arms over his chest, he stared at her.

She didn't stand a chance. She wilted under his stare. One thing his father did not share was Lachlan's ability to make his eyes cold as stone when needed. His father was too... nice.

"There's a rumor," she blurted.

He raised one eyebrow. "Go on."

"Did you really offer Old Widow McKeel sex in exchange for veterinarian services?"

Lachlan stared at her. His mind was not computing what she said. His brows furrowed and his eyes grew even harder.

"What?" He ground out. If he clenched his teeth any tighter, they'd crack.

"She's been telling everyone when you went to her farm to check on Donovan that she offered to pay you and you said you would take sex as payment. Even went so far as to trap her against the horse stall door."

Lachlan took several deep breaths. "That will be all, Donna. Please return to your desk."

22

"Yes, sir," she looked down at her fidgeting fingers. "For the record, sir, I don't believe her, but I wouldn't think differently about you if it did happen. You're young and single."

"I am not single. I'm a widower. Dear God, this is exactly why I left this place in the first place. The small mindedness and gossip, it is too much." He bit back the words as soon as he said them. He hadn't meant to take it out on her. She didn't deserve his ire. "I'm... sorry, Donna. Thank you for not believing her. It is a falsity and I will set the record straight."

She nodded but he could tell by her bowed head and hunched shoulders, he had stepped over the line. She moved past him and opened the door, only to jump in surprise.

"Oh, doctor," she greeted the person on the other side of the door with a genuine smile. "You gave me a fright. It's good to see you, sir. Can I make you a cup of tea?"

"Ah, thank you, Donna only you and my wife know how to make it perfectly. Sorry for the scare."

"Oh, no trouble and it's my pleasure, sir," she moved out of Lachlan sight and he locked eyes with his father.

Donna had never offered to make *him* a cup of tea and he liked it exactly the same way as his father. Maybe she believed more of the rumor than she let on. He scoffed, stopped himself from thinking anymore about it, and moved to his desk chair.

"What is it, da'?"

"Heya, son," his father's forced jovialness grated on his nerves. "Quiet today."

"Slow day for patients, I agree. But work never ends. Is there something I can help you with?" Lachlan was dangerously close to crossing a line with his tone, but he couldn't stop himself. "Or are you here to gloat that my practice isn't as thriving as yours?"

Cabhan's eyes grew stormy and he took a deep breath, puffing out his chest. Though his stance was still calm, his face told Lachlan he had just crossed a line.

"Tea, doctor?" Donna's voice came from behind him. In a flash, Cabhan's face relax into a smile as he turned to his former secretary.

"Ah, Donna, cheers," he took the teacup and sniffed. "Mmm, perfect. Thank you. Go ahead and close the door, Donna. My son and I are going to have a wee chat."

Lachlan had to consciously prevent his body from squirming when he heard the true meaning behind his father's words.

"Yes, sir," she glanced at Lachlan but did not wait for his approval before doing as his father bade. Something he would need to speak to her about later. Cabhan waited until the door was firmly closed before turning back to his son.

"You watch your tone with me, lad. You may be thirty-eight, but I will still take my hand to your arse if you disrespect me." His voice was calm, but the words were like ice.

Lachlan sighed and leaned back in his chair. "I'm sorry, da'. I'm beyond frustrated."

His father nodded once, and he knew all was forgiven. Cabhan took the seat opposite and drank his tea. "What really happened at Old McKeel's place? I don't believe that old slag for a minute."

"Well, obviously some do," Lachlan said.

"She's done this before, so soon people will start to catch on. She may as well install a revolving door in that gate of hers, it would be easier access for every man she has."

"You really don't like her, do you?"

Cabhan sighed. "You're much too young to remember this but she nearly cost me your mother."

"What?" Lachlan asked.

"She called me out, must have been twenty-five years ago now, to look at Donovan sire. Old McKeel had just died. There was nothing wrong with the horse, but she cornered me and got lipstick on my collar. I got out of there as fast as I could, but she spread a rumor around town that I had taken advantage of her grief. Your mother was pregnant with your brother Oisín, your Aunt Ness and Uncle Sean had just gotten married, you remember?"

Lachlan thought back to when he was thirteen and nodded.

"Well, Rachael never believed the rumor, but she found my shirt and demanded to know what happened. It took some convincing, but she believed me eventually," Cabhan explained.

"I don't remember that," Lachlan admitted.

"How could you? You were a boy."

"Well, she did something similar. Called me out to take a look at Donovan and took her top off."

"Blimey," his father breathed. "Did you gag? The woman's got to be ancient."

"She's younger than you, da'," Lachlan's voice was droll.

"Don't tell me you…"

"God no!" Lachlan exclaimed. "I told her I wasn't interested and left."

Cabhan nodded. "Typical."

"This was the first I'm hearing about any rumors though. Donna acts like she's scared of me."

"Donna is a saint. She put up with me for forty years," Cabhan said. "You just need to smile more and thank her."

"She doesn't offer to make me tea," he grumbled.

Cabhan laughed. "Well, once you start acting more like a human, she'll warm up to you. Trust me, you need to build a relationship with her. She can make your life hell," he chuckled.

"I'll try."

"I know you will." Cabhan finished his tea and leaned forward resting his hand on his son's arm. "Your mother and I worry about you, Lach. Come to dinner tonight. Stay over."

"I can't, da', not yet. It's too close to the…"

When he didn't continue, Cabhan finished, "The cemetery?" Lachlan nodded. "Have you gone since you've been back?"

"No," his voice was hard.

"Come with us to mass on Sunday, you can see it then."

"No, da', you know I can't do that. I don't believe anymore."

"God still believes in you," Cabhan said. Lachlan leaned back and extracted his arm out from under his father's hand.

"I'm sorry, but my answer has not changed."

"All right, I won't push," Cabhan stood to leave. "We always put two roses on the headstone. Every Sunday for you."

Lachlan's throat grew tight like someone was squeezing the life from him. "Thank you," he squeaked out. Cabhan headed to the door. "Da'," Lachlan called him back. "What do I do about

McKeel?"

"All you can do, prove her wrong."

"How?"

"Get her to acknowledge it in an open space."

"Make a scene?"

Cabhan shrugged. "You are the wounded party here. Get her to admit it."

"Will the practice survive?"

Cabhan looked confused, then laughed. "It's weathered much worse than this, believe me. Besides didn't you hear?"

"Here what?"

"About the hurricane."

"What hurricane?"

His father stared at him for a long second. "Dear God, we need to get you a telly. Hurricane Tyrone. It's only been on every two minutes. Making landfall tonight. Everyone's been making plans. Honestly, I was surprised you were here. Thought you would be at home making preparations. You are right by the water."

"There's a hurricane coming?" Lachlan questioned, turning in his chair to look out the window behind him where there were clouds, but the sun was still bright. "Isn't it a little early? It's only April."

"Either way, it's coming and making landfall by eleven tonight. Do you have food and water?"

"I have whiskey and crisps. I'll be fine."

Cabhan shook his head. "Might close up early, swing by

home." He held up his hand when Lachlan began to protest. "You won't stay long. We can go in through the back. You won't see the cemetery. I'm sure your mother stocked up enough for you too."

"Well, with no patients, I'll go ahead and leave with you. Get Donna home to her family," Lachlan stood, turned off his light, and left his office.

Chapter Five

"Now, do you have your ticket?" Geoff asked for the tenth time.

"Yes, I'll be fine." Corinne replied.

"I still don't know why you didn't want to fly," Geoff shook his head.

"You know I hate heights and the cost was three times the price of the ferry."

"Yeah, but it's faster."

"Honestly, I'll be fine. Thank you for everything." She

hugged him tightly.

"You have the new phone?" Geoff asked. Corinne pulled out the smartphone, burner phone Geoff had picked up earlier that day.

Oscar, crated beside her, looked up at her with sad, dark eyes.

"It's only for a couple minutes," she spoke softly to her hound. Oscar huffed and lowered his head to his paws. Looking back at Geoff, she saw the indecision and worry in his eyes. "Hey, I'll be all right. Thanks to you."

He nodded. "I just worry. That hurricane is coming, and I don't like the idea of you driving across the country while it's raining cats and dogs."

Oscar looked up but did nothing.

"I know," Corinne replied. "But it'll be fine. The hostel is right on Main Street, I can't miss it."

"Don't sell yourself short, love," he teased. She playfully smacked his arm. He grinned, then sobered and wrapped his arms around her. "Be safe. Listen to your instincts. Follow your gut. You got this, Cor."

She nodded and clamped her lips tight, feeling the telltale prick of tears. "I'll see you soon," she promised.

"I'll keep you updated on my dad's progress."

"I still can't believe you talked to him for me," she said.

"Hey," he cupped her jaw. "I love you. Of course I talked to him. I'd do anything for you."

"I love you, too, Geoff. Thank you for always being there."

"Always, love, now get going. Call me, yeah?"

The voice over the public address system advised they were boarding. Corinne embrace Geoff once more, picked up her duffel bag, one of Geoff's since hers was bright yellow and his, a muted military green, and took the handle of Oscar's wheeled crate. Walking to the ferry, she looked back. Geoff waved at her and blew her a kiss. She was ready.

Entering the ship, she quickly dropped off Oscar at the kennel and made her way up to the main deck. The ship was huge. There was a full restaurant, an arcade, a gift shop, bar, movie theater, kid area, they thought of everything. Not usually a drinker, except for the occasional white wine with Geoff, she made her way to the bar, near the gift shop.

"Hiya, what can I get for you?" The bartender greeted.

"A white wine please, dry," she ordered.

The bartender turned away to fill the order and she had a moment to catch her breath.

"Make that two," a man said walking up and leaning on the bar to her right. She looked over, her stomach somewhere near her feet. She breathed easier when the man gave her a smile and was most definitely not Anthony Rossi. "Nervous traveler?" he asked.

She forced a smile to be polite. "First time, actually."

"Really? Oh, I travel all the time. Everywhere."

"That sounds tedious," she blurted. "Sorry, I sometimes say exactly what's on my mind even if it's rude. I apologize."

"No, no, you're absolutely right. It is tedious. But there are some things that help break up the tedium."

"Such as?"

"Meeting beautiful women like yourself for starters.

31

Buying them drinks," he gave the bartender some cash, "and asking to sit with them to get to know them."

"The crossing is only two hours."

"You'd be surprised what you can learn about someone in two hours," he said clinking his glass to hers.

She hesitated and he looked down at her arm holding a book to her chest. "I guess talking wasn't what you had in mind, is it?" She shrugged. "I get it. Hey, it isn't the first time I've been beaten out by a book and I'm sure it won't be the last."

"Are you sure?"

"Absolutely," he agreed. "Enjoy your wine, maybe I'll see you in a bit."

"All right, thanks and thank you for the wine. I can pay you—"

He waved a hand. "Forget about it. Enjoy."

She thanked him and headed to one of the chairs by the window.

An hour went by and the book engrossed her. She didn't lift her eyes from the pages until she drank the last of her wine. Coming to a stop in the story was harder than she thought it would be. She winced when she raised her head and felt how stiff her neck was. Leaning back in her chair, she filled her lungs which oddly ached too from being confined as she hunched over the table.

Her eyes scanned the water outside, seeing the small whitecaps as the choppy waves broke against more water. Her gaze pulled back and she looked around the room. A mother scolded her children for running around, a couple spoke closely together, and several businessmen in suits laughed together.

She looked further to her left and saw the same man from earlier sipping a full glass of white wine while reading on his phone. Their eyes locked and he instantly smiled. *What the hell,* she thought. Standing, she gathered her things along with the empty wine glass and headed his way. He leaned back in the chair, his smile growing with every step she took.

"Book not interesting enough?" He questioned.

"Book is plenty interesting, but so are you," she replied.

A twinkle appeared in his eyes. "I'm glad to hear you say that." His eyes dropped to the empty glass in her hands. "Can I get you a refill?"

"Thanks," she answered. He gestured to the seat beside him and took her glass to the bar.

Chapter Six

Don't look, don't look, don't look. Breathe, breathe, breathe, don't look. Lachlan repeated the mantra in his head as they got closer to his parent's house. His father was speaking but he tuned him out. He could only hear the rush of blood in his ears and the *pound, pound, pound* of his heart beating. His hands grew sweaty and his mouth went dry.

His parents lived near the church every member of his family attended for generations. But along with the church, there was a cemetery. And in that cemetery, was his wife and daughter.

He jumped out of his skin when his father's hand came down on his shoulder. Cabhan watched him but nodded slowly.

"We're here, lad, no need to torture yourself further. In and out and back to your cottage."

Lachlan nodded and, with a deep breath, he followed his father into the house.

Corinne couldn't stop her smile as she drove. She was sorrier than she thought she would be when the ferry docked and her conversation with… George, was over.

He was such an interesting man. He had traveled all over the world and still found time to volunteer at an animal shelter in North Wales, where he lived.

She was sorry she had chosen the book over him at first. Though, Keera O'Shea's latest thriller was definitely a page turner. Still, she beamed, she had gotten his number and called him to give him her new number before they parted. She sent a text to Geoff before she started the rental.

Corinne: Landed safe and sound. Will call when I reach the hostel. Have something fun to tell you.

She was giddy. Finally, getting out there, following her gut… Geoff would be proud. She wanted to call him, but the first of the hurricane was rolling in and the clouds grew darker by the minute. Wanting to get on the road, she checked the address was in her GPS as Geoff's reply came in.

Geoff: So glad you made it safe, love. Call me soon. Fun news is always welcome. Be safe. That storm looks bad.

As if in answer to his text, thunder rumbled. Oscar whined in the backseat. Clearly, his animal sense told him a massive storm was eminent.

"It's all right, boy, we'll be fine," she soothed but her fingers gripped the steering wheel tighter as the light rain began. Her knuckles turned white.

Lachlan stood in his parent's kitchen, arms out, already laden with food, toiletries, a case of water, milk, bread, and every canned item he could think of. His mother was in the pantry, muttering about "that one thing" she bought for him. His father and baby brother, Oisín looked on in amusement.

"Ah ha!" She cried *eureka* and pulled out a box of candles, matches, and a small oil lamp. "There we go."

Lachlan heard his father and brother snicker. He didn't have electricity at his cottage. He was never there so why pay for it? He had a whole month's supply of candles, oil, and lamps. But he wasn't about to mention that to his mother.

"Cheers, ma," he answered.

"Now, do you have everything you need?" she asked.

"And then some, thanks to you," he replied.

"Well, they say it's already a cat four and could elevate to a cat five by the time it hits. They say the storm surge will cause damage. It's set to be the worst storm Ireland's seen in decades. Now, I do wish you'd stay with us. You are right by the sea."

The thought of sleeping in the same bed he slept in the night before his wedding, the bed he and Karin shared whenever they stayed over, caused bile to fill his mouth.

"He'll be fine, love," his father stepped forward saving him. "Leave him be. He's at least on the hilltop not at sea level."

"True, oh darling, promise me you'll be careful!"

"I promise, ma, and thanks to all of this, I'll be set until the roads reopen," Lachlan replied, proud of how level his voice was.

"All right, darling, call us as soon as the phones are working to let us know how things are," she said.

"I will," he promised as they walked to the door. Lachlan was surprised how quickly the clouds had darkened. He'd only been in his parent's house for twenty minutes but already the sky threatened rain and he could smell his most hated scent: Petrichor, the same he smelled ten years ago and one he always associated with the worst day of his life, his wife's and child's funeral.

"Do you need help carrying it all?" She finally asked as they reached the door. Breaking him out of his lament, he was about to reply when she turned to his brother. "Oisín, help your brother."

"See, I would, ma but I pulled something on my last move, ow!" She had smacked his arm with the wooden spoon in her apron pocket.

"If you don't help him, I'll make sure you pull something. Now, do as you're told," she ordered.

"Geez, ma, okay, I'm going," he rubbed his arm. Lachlan was sure it still stung. Their mother wouldn't hurt a fly, unless that fly was one of her children talking back to her. Oisín was a safe distance away from the spoon when he looked at Lachlan and rolled his eyes. Lachlan bit back a laugh, only to realize it would have been the first genuine laugh he gave since Karin died.

Oisín took one of the loaves of bread and turned back to his mother. "See? I'm helping."

Cabhan laughed outright and shook his head. "You are dangerously close to getting a whoopin', lad."

"I'm twenty-five."

"Aye, old enough to know better," their mother said.

"Fine, here," he grinned and offered to take the lot. Lachlan gladly gave it to him as his arms were already shaking from the strain. He was hardly weak, being a vet, Lachlan sometimes needed muscle to move an animal that weighed ten times him, but in sheer brute strength, his six-foot six-inch *baby* brother had him beat.

"Get home soon," Cabhan called, his eyes in the darkening clouds. "Remember, Lach," he looked back at his son. "An oil lamp in the front room window, it's a sign to any traveler you are a medical man."

"Aye, I remember," he said.

"And no stopping at the pub on the way back, Oisín."

"Ah, come on, da'," he whined.

"Straight back, do you hear me?" Cabhan stated.

"Aye, fine," Oisín's shoulders slumped.

"Once the storm's over, I'll join you for a pint if you want," Lachlan offered.

"Aye, gladly," Oisín smiled.

He and his brother started walking down the main road leading to Lachlan's cottage. Only three miles each way, Lachlan usually walked from home to the office and their parent's house was closer still. Lachlan didn't envy Oisín on the steep uphill incline as they started.

"I didn't get a chance to properly thank you and your friends for moving me in so easily, Osh," Lachlan said.

"No worries," Oisín replied. "It was one of the easiest moves we've done. You didn't really have that much stuff."

"Still, I'm grateful."

"I appreciate that, Lach, and I'm glad you're back. I know why you left and I'm sorry for it... Damn sorry, but I'm glad you're back. I hope we can get to know each other again."

"You may not like who I am now," Lachlan said.

"I may yet," Oisín answered.

"I hope so because I don't see me changing.

They were quiet for a long moment.

"I see you still wear your ring," Oisín said cautiously.

"Yes." His hand suddenly felt heavy.

"Can I..." he cleared his throat. "Can I ask why? It's been ten years."

"You can always ask me anything," he answered. "I wear it because it feels wrong to take it off. It would send a message I'm not ready for. I loved her, *love* her, so much. I want to show our love to the world and that means wearing the ring she gave me."

"Don't you think it's a little... living in the past, like? A little somber?"

"I prefer to think of it as a remembrance."

"But you can't honestly expect to pick up women while wearing that thing. I mean, unless they are into that."

"I don't intend to pick up women at all."

Oisín looked at him like he had just grown another head. "You can't be serious."

"As serious as I ever am," Lachlan stated.

"You are going to be celibate for the rest of your life?" Oisín looked like he had just swallowed a bug.

"I don't see why not."

Oisín coughed. "Seriously?"

"There is more to life than that. Trust me, I was your age once and married to the love of my life. I know what you mean but now… there's no point."

"She wouldn't want you to be living in the past. She would want you to move on and be the man she loved."

Lachlan forced a smile. His brother was saying what everyone else had said. But he didn't care what everyone thought his Karin would say, *she* didn't say it, that was all that mattered. The cottage came into view and he stopped.

"I can take it if you want to go back. You might even be able to get that pint in before it starts," he eyed the clouds.

"Ha! And have da' smell it on my breath? No, thank you, my poor arm can't take anymore from ma's spoon, like."

Lachlan breathed a laugh and walked on. His brother's arms were huge and could easily take a *beating* from their mother's wooden spoon. But he wasn't going to say anything and besides, the clouds looked to be getting darker by the minute and the sea was beginning to get restless.

Unlocking his door, he let his brother in first, gave him a quick hug once he had set the box down, and watched as Oisín walked down the path.

"Just remember, Lach, selkies come to shore with the storm. Don't be taken in by their pretty faces," he called over his shoulder.

"I'm not the one who needs to be warned about pretty faces, Oisín," Lachlan called back and chuckled.

Like a muscle that hadn't been exercised in a while, his chuckle came out harsher than he meant but it was a step forward he had to celebrate. Seeing his brother's retreating form jog down the hill toward his parent's house, Lachlan drew back inside just as large drops started and the thunder rumbled. One thing was clear, he pitied anyone, man or beast who would be outside that night.

Lighting a few candles, he made sure to light an oil lamp and put it in the front windowsill. Then, he cooked something quickly on the wood-burning stove for dinner. The wind whipped around him, and the old cottage groaned as it became darker and darker. More candles and a glass of whiskey in hand, Lachlan sat in his chair and took his Aunt Keera's latest book.

Rain pelted the windows and roof, but it didn't worry him. The old cottage had stood the test of time and weathered many a storm. He was just finishing the book and about to seek his bed, when a ruckus outside his main door drew his attention. He stopped and listened.

He could have sworn he heard something out there. Then a voice, and someone pounding on his door, echoed.

"Hello? Hello, is anyone there? Please, I need help!"

Lachlan jumped up and raced to the door. Opening it, the wind blew in and blew out the few candles in its way.

Looking down at the person needing help, all he could see for a moment was a figure wearing jeans and a shirt, both soaked through, but the hood of the raincoat hid the face until lightning streaked across the sky and illuminated her.

Lachlan felt his entire nice, neat, self-pitying world crumble.

The woman was beautiful and scared. Another lightning bolt struck, but not across the sky that time, instead figuratively it was right to his heart, causing that organ to slowly start pumping again.

He swallowed hard at the pleasure-pain. So that was the feeling his grandfather Orin always talked about. The feeling of life flowing again. The feeling to prove, even after someone you love died, you are not dead yet no matter how much you wish to be.

"Please, can you help me?" she begged, her voice bringing him back. "It's my dog, he's hurt!"

Shaking out of his surprised stupor, Lachlan wasted no more time. He grabbed his raincoat, not that it would do much good, the wind blew fiercely, and the storm had yet to make landfall. Grabbing his bag, he hurried outside and followed the woman, the siren. If he didn't know better, he would have believed his brother's joke had come true and she was a selkie, blown in from the sea. Shaking his head, he turned his focus on what needed him, the dog.

Chapter Seven

No no no, this couldn't be happening! Corinne had let Oscar out to pee before the rain got any harder.

But as soon as she got back in the car, the engine wouldn't start. She was only three miles from Main Street and five miles, according to her GPS, to the hostel. But she was already past the time she wanted to arrive, as she drove slower in the rain. Checking her phone, she let out a sob when the *no service* icon appeared, and the GPS searched for a signal.

"Please! Come on!" she cried.

Lightning streaked across the sky making her scream.

Oscar barked, his tail between his legs.

"I know, boy, I know." She grabbed his big head between her hands and kissed his forehead. "It's going to be okay. I promise. I'll get us to safety." The wind was blowing so hard that the little rental car she had gotten at the dock, shook back and forth. "We can't stay here." She looked Oscar in the eyes. "We have to find shelter." He licked her nose in agreement. "But where?" she whispered looking out the window at the massive storm.

Fortunately, before her radio cut out two miles back, she had heard the hurricane dropped to a category two, but still, the wind was nightmarishly strong.

"Okay," she breathed. "Come on, Oscar. We need to go."

Opening her door, she shrieked when the wind nearly took it off its hinges. Oscar barked and jumped out too. When the lightning streaked, she looked all around her. The road went to her right and left, the ocean before her. As her car was pointed toward the left, she decided to try that way.

It didn't take long for her jeans and trainers to be soaked. Her t-shirt plastered to her chest. Oscar trotted right beside her.

They had to hurry. Corinne started to jog, but there were no houses, no sign of life anywhere and then it happened. She stopped when she heard the creaking, then a loud snap. And then, her heart stopped, as Oscar yelped.

"Oscar?" she screamed. Lightning struck and she saw her dog, her beloved companion, pinned underneath a large branch. "Oscar!" she shrieked.

Rushing to him, lightning struck again, and she saw the top of a pine tree had fallen and trapped Oscar under its weight. His little face looked up at her, almost resigned, but she cried and held on to him. "I'll get you out!" she swore. Grabbing a branch, she strained but couldn't raise it. The weight, wind, and rain were too much for her. Oscar looked up at her, pain in his dark eyes.

Lightning streaked again and in the bright light she saw a lone cottage in the distance.

"Oscar," she turned back to him. "I will be right back. Look, boy, look. See? I'm going right there. I will be right back. I promise!"

He licked her hand and she stood. Rushing forward, she tripped and fell, crying out. Oscar barked.

"I'm okay," she called back to her wolfhound. Standing, she winced when she put pressure on her twisted ankle, but she hurried to the door, a single lamp lit in the front window. Somewhere in the back of her mind she remembered her mother mentioning that was a symbol in Ireland of a medical professional.

The wind propelled her to the door. Pounding on it, she hoped her cries were heard above the wind. For Oscar's sake, she hoped the person inside was willing to help.

"What happened?" Lachlan demanded over the wind and rain.

"The top of a pine tree snapped and pinned him down," she sounded shrill and scared. No time to understand why he wanted to pull her to him and comfort her, he turned his attention to the fallen tree and the whimpering dog beneath it.

"What's his name?" He called.

"Oscar," she replied.

"Oscar, it's all right, lad." Even though many thought it silly, Lachlan always learned the names of the animals, speaking to them as if they understood. In his experience, they often did.

Assessing the situation, he knew most everyone's initial reaction would be to lift the tree immediately, but that could cause more injury. To make sure it was safe to lift blind, Lachlan found the dog's head, slid his hands down its neck, under the tree and further across the animal's back and belly. That's when he felt it.

"Shite," he muttered. One of the tree's limbs had punctured between the ribs. *Not good.* It was too close to his spleen.

"What's wrong?" she questioned.

"Nothing," he answered.

"Don't sugarcoat it," she snapped.

"There's a puncture," he replied.

"Where?"

"On the side by his belly."

"Liver or spleen?"

Lachlan's eyes widened. "Spleen."

"Oh god! Oscar, it'll be okay." The dog had lost consciousness. "Can I apply pressure while you lift the tree?"

"We need to be quick. We have to get him back to my cottage."

"We will," she was determined. "I'm a vet tech, if it helps. I can assist."

Lachlan nodded. That made sense. She was knowledgeable of anatomy and he could do with her help.

"In my bag," he motioned with his head beside him. "Are gauze strips. I don't want to lose the location." His hands were still around the branch. The woman didn't hesitate. She rushed to his other side, opened the bag, and found the gauze.

"Hurry. I don't want it to get too wet."

She nodded and sheltered the strips under her coat. Lachlan took her hand and guided it to the injury. She squeaked a moan. "Oh, Oscar, I'm so sorry."

Lachlan again had no time to wonder at the feelings stirring inside him. "I'm going to lift, on three." he said. She nodded.

Getting under the largest part of the tree, he counted and lifted. Oscar whimpered. *Good, he's conscious.* Lachlan grunted as he moved the tree to the other side. Moving as quickly as he could, he grabbed his bag and hurried over to Oscar and the woman. Scooping Oscar in his arms, he carried him. The woman was rushing beside him, the gauze still in her hand pressed to Oscar, the amount of blood worried him. They had nothing for a transfusion.

Ignoring the soft sounds of the interesting woman beside him as she limped, he nearly ran to his cottage. The woman opened the door and Lachlan's eyes fell on the dining table.

"Clear that table," he ordered.

She did as he bid and cradled Oscar's head as Lachlan set him down. "Easy, lad," he soothed.

"What do you need?" she questioned.

"In the bag, pull out the sedative and give me twenty milligrams." He lifted his hands for two precious seconds to shrug out of his raincoat. The woman was by his side with the filled syringe. "It's all right, Oscar," Lachlan soothed as he injected the sedative. It took effect almost immediately with Oscar going still but for the rise and fall of his breathing. "I need to check if there are any splinters and how bad the wound is."

"Tell me what you need."

They continued until Lachlan was positive the wound was not deep enough nor near enough to any vital organs. Oscar would be all right. Finally, after sewing up the wound, he wrapped the dog's middle. The woman stroked the dog's head and kissed him. Once done, Lachlan moved away, washed his hands, and lit more candles, it was going to be a long night.

He poured a whiskey, topped off the wood in the stove, and walked over to the woman.

"Here, drink this, you're wet through," he offered the alcohol.

"Thanks," she answered and took a sip, shuddering when she drank it down. "Thank you for saving him. I was fortunate to find you. Are you a doctor?"

"Veterinarian," he replied.

She smiled. "My lucky day. Thank you."

He nodded and drank his whiskey. "What happened?" He asked.

"My car wouldn't start. I was heading to town to the hostel when I let Oscar out, not sure if we would get another chance with the weather the way it was, I tried the key in the engine and it wouldn't turn over. I knew we couldn't stay there, we have yet to get to the major part of the storm. We were walking toward town."

Lachlan nodded, then realized they were both soaked. "You have luggage in the car?"

She nodded looking down at her clothes. "I'll be dry soon enough."

"Wait here?"

She agreed and he walked toward the back of the cottage to his bedroom.

He set his whiskey on the dresser and pulled out of his shirt and jeans. In nothing but his skin, he dug around in the drawer finding dry clothes.

"Doctor?" To his horror, he heard her voice then she gasped. He whirled around. Her eyes dropped to his chest and invariably lower, then she snapped her eyes shut and squeaked. Immediately, he covered his lower parts with a t-shirt and sweatpants but not before she got a good look. There was something almost endearing to him about how she didn't stare and how her cheeks turned pink.

"I'm so sorry but Oscar's fussing."

Lachlan nodded once but didn't move. She cracked one eye open then closed it again. "I'll leave. Sorry."

He waited until she was gone to move and then quickly as he could, he dressed. Grabbing an extra pair of sweatpants and a shirt he had pulled out of the dresser, he walked down the hall to where he saw the woman, he had yet to ask her name, standing over her dog, an Irish wolfhound Lachlan had recognized, who was whimpering.

"Shh, it's all right, love," she soothed and began humming a song to him. Lachlan couldn't make his feet work. Her voice was so soothing and something about it made Lachlan smile, his first genuine smile since Karin died.

The woman looked up at him, her cheeks turning pink. It was clear what she was remembering. Lachlan stepped forward and offered the extra pair of sweats.

"I'll take care of Oscar. These will be too big but you're welcome to change. Bathroom is through there."

"Thank you," she said.

She walked past him, still limping and accepted the clothes

but didn't look him in the eyes.

"Wait," he called her back. She turned. "I'm sorry about earlier."

"Oh, no, you have nothing to apologize for. You asked me to stay put and I didn't. I intruded. I just hope your wife will understand."

Lachlan started, his brows coming together. "My wife?" She looked pointedly down to his left hand. He breathed deeply but nodded. "She would." The woman smiled but turned again. "What's your name?" He blurted out.

She turned again. "Corinne," she answered. Then, with a smile, left the room.

"Corinne," he whispered, a smile lifting his lips.

Chapter Eight

Oh my God, oh my God, oh my God. Why did I go after him? What was I thinking?

Seeing Lachlan completely nude was a shock, but she didn't stare, she couldn't. She had seen his gold wedding band as he helped Oscar. Now she was alone, her thoughts drifted back to what she had seen. She remembered every detail, her cheeks heating.

His wife was an incredibly lucky lady. He was well built, though his stomach muscles were not as defined as other's, he was trim and handsome. His dark brown hair with some grey, gave him a sexy appeal, but his eyes... it looked like he had not smiled nor laughed in years. There was something behind his eyes she couldn't place.

Then, she froze. She didn't know his name. He asked her hers, but she didn't think to ask his. All she could think about, was getting out of his line of sight so she could blush in peace.

She wondered what his name could be. Typical Irish names came to her, but none seemed to fit him. The wind howled and beat against the walls and roof. She yelped when thunder crashed so loudly at rattled her teeth.

"Corinne?" The doctor called and raced into the bathroom. She had just pulled on the new clothes but seeing the worried look in his eyes made her sob. "Are you all right?" He asked stepping into the room. She let everything go. All the emotions from the past couple days, everything. A sob escaped and she could not stop her tears. The doctor reached forward, and she fell into his arms, crying. Everything that had happened, the fear, the hurt, the worry, the fear for Oscar, her dislike of storms, everything.

The doctor held her to him, his soothing voice calming her. Finally, her tears subsided, and she looked up at him. He leaned back to look at her and smiled, stroking her hair away from her face. She locked eyes with his tortured toffee colored ones and instinctively leaned forward. The doctor pulled away and his brows furrowed.

"I'm sorry," she gasped and leaned back, putting much needed distance between them.

"It's all right," he answered. "You're scared and vulnerable. I hope you know I would never take advantage of that."

"Thank you," she replied. "I hope your wife is understanding," she said and again she saw something pass behind his eyes, making her wonder. "Is she out there in this?"

"No," he answered. "Well, sort of."

"Sort of?" She questioned then shook her head and raised her hand. "I'm sorry, none of my business."

"No, it's not, but it's fine," he answered. She blushed again.

"Sorry, what's your name? Or would you rather I just call you *doctor*?"

"Not needed," he assured. "My name is Lachlan."

Lachlan... she grinned. That fit him perfectly. "Lachlan," she said. "Thank you for helping me and thank you so much for saving Oscar."

"You're welcome," his deep baritone voice raised goosebumps on her skin. They walked back out to the main room. "You're limping." He looked down at her foot.

"I tripped running here," she admitted. "I'm okay."

"Sit, let me get you some ice." He pushed the ottoman over to a wingback chair and helped her lift her bare foot. "Let me take a look?"

"Sure," she agreed, and he rolled up her pant leg.

"Does this hurt?" he prodded an area, but she shook her head. "Good, it's a little swollen, but nothing seems torn or broken." He set her foot back down on the footrest. "I'll grab some ice for you."

She watched him head into the kitchen as the wind howled outside. "Do you know when the storm is supposed to end?"

"The eye makes landfall around three, at least that's what they said. The remnants will probably stick around until well into tomorrow."

"I just wanted to get my things from the car but don't want to get soaked again and maybe get to the hostel," she said.

"Oscar should not be moved until at least day after tomorrow," Lachlan replied walking back out of the kitchen with some ice wrapped in a towel. "I want to monitor him tonight. Maybe we can take shifts?"

"That'd be fine," she answered as he crouched before her and held the ice on her ankle. Shaking out another towel, he wrapped it around her ankle and the ice, tying it so the compress stayed in place. "Thank you."

"You're welcome. You and Oscar can stay here until it's safe to travel."

"I couldn't possibly put you out."

"You aren't," he assured. "My ma gave me too much food for just me. You'd be welcome."

"Just you? When is your wife coming home?"

Lachlan swallowed and looked away. Corinne sunk her teeth into her lower lip. She had inadvertently offended him.

"I'm sorry if I…"

"My wife is dead," he grunted and turned to look at her again.

Corinne's breath caught in her throat seeing the tears gather in his beautiful eyes, then vanish.

"I wear this," he raised his hand showing the ring. "To remember her by. I know you didn't know, but it would help me to have you stop mentioning her."

"I'm so sorry, I didn't—"

"I know."

"Can I ask when?"

"Ten years ago."

"I'm sorry. But that is wonderful that you still remember and honor her. I can see you loved her very much."

His brows furrowed. "That's not what people usually say."

"What do they usually say?"

"Move on."

Corinne shook her head. "No, you move on if and when *you* want to. Not on their timeline. I've seen it too often. When people lose a pet and get another too fast, it's difficult on them and the pet... not that losing your wife is like losing a pet, and I'm not trying to compare her to an animal, um."

Chapter Nine

Lachlan had to hold in his chuckle, one he never thought he would do again. Corinne was floundering but he couldn't bring himself to be upset or even offended. Coming from anyone else, he would have bitten their head off with a few choice words. But with her, Lachlan merely wanted to watch her and listen. Her words made sense, in a way.

Earlier, when she had almost kissed him, he pulled back out of respect for her and the memory of his wife, not the other way around and that worried him. This woman was getting to him, burrowing deeper than anyone had been able to before. That stupid lightning feeling simply made it more difficult.

"Corinne," he stopped her, taking pity. "It's all right. I know what you meant. Now, how about a sandwich? You probably haven't eaten, have you?" She shook her head. "Then let me give you something and I'll put on a pot of coffee. Any dietary restrictions?"

She nodded. "I can't have shellfish."

"Okay, how about a BLT?" He asked.

Her stomach immediately growled, and Lachlan smiled. "Sounds good," she said.

"Good, watch Oscar for me?"

She nodded and her eyes drifted to her dog. Lachlan rounded the corner to his kitchen and took a deep heavy breath. He realized almost too late it was the deepest breath without pain he had taken in ten years. The woman was worrying him. *What is this feeling?* He wondered.

Shrugging off the wall he had leaned against, he opened the pantry and the small ice box he kept so he didn't have to have a refrigerator. Pulling out the bacon, he grabbed the produce he needed and a pan. When he moved in three months ago, he had the previous owners take the old gas stove with them and he replaced it with a wood burning one. Oisín, his brother, sometimes teased him saying how he was surprised Lachlan had agreed to have running water for the toilets and not just use a chamber pot.

As the bacon fried, he grabbed some coffee and brewed a pot. Most of his family preferred tea but ever since Lachlan was in school, he always swore by coffee. One thing his cousin, Trevor and he shared, but then, Trevor was half-American, and God knew Americans always loved their coffee.

The bacon was ready, and Lachlan built the sandwiches, adding some spicy sauce for his. Karin had been half Mexican and loved making and eating spicy foods, something she introduced to

Lachlan and he enjoyed still. Pouring two cups of coffee, he placed everything on a tray and carried it to the living room.

Corinne looked up from her phone when he came in.

"You probably won't have service," he said. "The storm makes it impossible." He gestured to his phone on the mantlepiece.

Corinne huffed a sigh and set the phone down. "I need to tell my friend I'm okay. He's a worrier."

"When the storm breaks, we can go to my parents. They have Wi-Fi… if it's working."

"I couldn't put you out," she said.

"No worries. They're only a mile. And they're closer to town."

"To the hostel?"

"Yeah, Mrs. Jacobson's place is on the High Street. You would have gone right past my parent's house. My brother has a business and lives with them, so they have to have an internet connection for him."

"Thanks," she said. "He will be worried sick if he doesn't hear from me."

"He sounds like a good friend," Lachlan sat down in the chair beside her and took the coffee.

"He is, it was actually his idea for me to come here."

Lachlan offered her the plate with the non-spicy sandwich. "What brings you here? No offense, but by your English accent you aren't from around here."

"London, born and bred."

"I'm sorry," Lachlan couldn't believe it. His tone was light, and he was actually teasing her. He hadn't teased any one in years. Corinne breathed a laugh and looked down.

"Mum was Irish, Dad's Scottish, so I can't claim any English blood."

"Thank Christ," Lachlan mumbled.

"You Irish really don't like the English, do you?"

"No," he replied simply.

"Well, it's a good thing my friend isn't here," she laughed. "He's not only English through and through, he's an aristocrat."

Lachlan chuckled. "That's two strikes against him. In the words of my American cousin, three and he's out."

She laughed again and Lachlan smiled. He liked the sound.

"No other strikes. He is the kindest, dearest, sweetest man alive."

"Are you two... together?" Something in his gut clinched when he asked.

"No," she shook her head. "Just best friends. Neither of us are attracted to each other. Besides, he is a playboy and philanderer. Not something I'm interested in long term."

"Oh, I see," Lachlan breathed easier. "Sorry."

"No, no, we would be married by now if he wasn't like that and if we actually did like each other that way. But he's betrothed since the woman was born. They'll have to marry soon. Aristocrats keep the bloodline in their society. We would never have worked out. He's more like a brother anyway," she looked up at him, horror written all over her face. "Oh, God I'm sorry."

"For what?" Then, he realized she had talked about

marriage, a topic he avoided like the plague. But he didn't know how to change the subject.

"My cousin's cousin, Peter, is engaged. He's an American. It doesn't bother me," he finally said. "Life goes on."

She looked over at him and smiled. "Thanks. When's the wedding?"

"Not sure. They're putting it off. Something about her job. I'm glad he's found someone. Vivian seems nice. I've only met her once."

"Vivian?" She questioned.

"Aye."

"Vivian and Peter… Carlisle?"

Lachlan froze as he looked at her. "Aye," he said slowly. "Do you know him?"

"Sort of," she replied. "Wow, what a small world. Um… He's Geoff's, that's my best friend, friend. Geoff recommended Ireland because he knew Peter has family here."

"Geoff… Geoffrey Ainsley?"

"The same."

"Well, I've met him once when he came with Peter to Trevor's final year musical. My cousin played the Phantom in the *Phantom of the Opera*."

"Oh wow, it really is a small world."

"Not really. You came to Kerry. You'll eventually meet one of us O'Quinns. As my Uncle Emmet says, we're a dynasty. But yes, Peter Carlisle is my cousin's cousin on his mother's side."

"So, not only were you here when I needed you, you are a

vet, and your family is my best friend's friend, the reason he told me to come here. Someone up there must be watching out for me."

"I've never thought so," Lachlan disagreed.

Corinne looked up at him briefly and looked down into her coffee.

"Sorry... God and I don't get along."

"I felt the same way when my mom died. But He's the only thing I could rely on. My dad's a drunk."

Lachlan let the subject die and they ate in silence. The burn of the hot sauce felt good. It dulled the ache that happened whenever he denied believing in a higher power. He, along with his cousin Trevor and his siblings were all altar boys at the local church his family attended for generations. Far too many O'Quinns were buried in the church yard. At least, two too many.

Her yawn brought him back to reality.

"Why don't you go and get some sleep?" He offered. "You've been through a lot."

"I am tired," she admitted.

"Go," he said, indicating the hallway. "Sorry, there's only one bed. The other room, I haven't set up yet. Take it. I'll be out here."

"Are you sure?"

"Yes," he answered. He needed her out of his sight to work through the feelings within him.

"When you need me to take over, let me know." She stood.

"I will, sleep well."

"Thank you, for everything."

"You're welcome. You're safe now."

There was a flash of something in her eyes, but it was gone before Lachlan could decipher it. He watched her walk down the hall and disappear into his room.

He sighed deeply, stood, and went to the pantry to retrieve more candles. He checked the oil lamp on the sill, glad to see it was still burning bright and the oil basin was still nearly full.

The storm raged outside, but it was the storm within him that worried him. For the past ten years, he felt nothing, either beating in his chest or below the belt. Now both seem to take notice of the beautiful woman. The fact she was sleeping in his bed... he blew out a breath.

"Easy," he grumbled, grabbing his coffee, and leaning back. He couldn't get attached. She would be gone in a couple days and he'd be alone... again.

Chapter Ten

Corinne was running as fast as she could. Rain pelted her face and the wind blew so fiercely she could barely push through. It was dark. There was no light, nothing but darkness, rain, wind. She pulled up with a screech when the path suddenly dropped off to a dramatic cliff. Her heart pounded as some of the pebbles at her feet fell over and bounced down the rocks.

Turning to look behind her, Anthony Rossi sauntered up, a cigar between his teeth, his stupid aviator glasses still covering his eyes.

"Well well, what do we have here?" He questioned and two of his men walked up beside him.

She was trapped.

"There's nowhere to run, Corinne. I always know where you are," he took a step toward her and she stepped back, catching herself before she slipped. He extended his hand to her. "You don't want to have your father killed, now do you?"

Glancing to her right, one of his men stood, cutting off that route. Then to her left. The other man blocked that way.

"I won't wait forever. He is as good as dead if you don't come with me now." He licked his thick lips and a shudder raced through her.

"No," she stated. "I'd rather die."

"You die, you'll take your father and Geoffrey with you, for I will kill them both."

She swallowed hard and the wind whipped about her. It wasn't worth Geoffrey's life. She couldn't risk it.

"No! Don't do it, Corinne!" Geoff's voice came from the wind.

"Geoff?" She called.

"Don't," he shouted again and that time, she heard a growl and scream. Her gaze darted to the man at the right. Oscar was on top of him clawing and biting. Looking to her left, Geoffrey was fighting the other man. Pulling her gaze back to Anthony in front of her, he pulled a gun and aimed.

"Bitch," he muttered and pulled the trigger.

Just then, a figure moved in front of her and took the bullet. The person fell at her feet and Anthony disappeared. Geoffrey and Oscar vanished, leaving only the crumpled figure on the ground. She fell to her knees and gently turned the person over to see who had taken the bullet meant for her.

She screamed when she recognized Lachlan's face.

"Corinne, wake up, it's okay," she heard someone say in her ear. Soon, the darkness abated, and she opened her eyes. Lachlan, alive, leaned over her, gently shaking her shoulders.

She threw her arms around him and hugged him. Tears tracked down her cheeks. She felt the surprise in his rigid body but after a moment he melted a little and wrapped his arms around her.

"It's all right. You're okay," he whispered.

Corinne slowed her breathing. It was a dream. Only a dream. But it could become reality and that meant Lachlan would be in danger if Anthony Rossi found out where she was. Even though she only met him a few hours ago, she couldn't let him be hurt. She needed to leave and soon. He would be safer that way.

"When can Oscar and I leave?" She felt him tense again and pulled back to look into his tortured, toffee colored eyes. She didn't want to hurt him, and he deserved the truth. "I haven't been entirely honest with you, Lachlan," she began. "I have some pretty dangerous men after me and I don't want anyone to get hurt, least of all you. You've been so kind to me."

He stared at her for a long moment, searching her eyes for something. She forced herself to hold his gaze and opened herself to him.

"That's why you're here? Why you were driving through a hurricane? Someone's after you?" He questioned. She nodded. "Who?"

What did it hurt? She wondered. "A man named Anthony Rossi. He is the son of Ricardo Rossi, a known mobster in London."

"What does he want with you?"

She looked down. She may hate what her father had done but he was still her father and she respected him.

"I can't protect you if I don't know everything, Corinne."

She snapped her gaze up to him. "Protect me?" she asked. "Why? You don't even know me."

"You're right. But that doesn't stop the fact you are here and I'm not about to let you go at this on your own."

She watched as his eyes changed from tortured to determined. She knew he needed the truth and for his safety, she needed to come clean. Slowly, she nodded. "All right," she agreed. "Can we go into the sitting room?"

"Of course," he stood from the bed and offered his hand to her. "I just made another pot of coffee."

She accepted his help up and walked with him to the living space.

"You're not limping as much," he observed.

"The ice really helped. Thank you," she said.

Oscar still lay on the table, sleeping. Lachlan had placed a rolled-up blanket under his head. Just seeing the soft rise and fall of his belly as he slept, caused tears to prick her eyes. He was her mother's. She had picked him up as a puppy, barely six weeks old on her last visit to Ireland. She died on his first birthday. Since then, Corinne took care of him and together they worked through her mother's death.

Lachlan came back from the kitchen with two mugs of coffee. Corinne watched him, almost numb. She would need to be numb for their coming conversation. He looked back at her and she realized he was waiting for her to join him and sit. Tucking her feet under her as she sat on the leather chair near the hearth, she took the mug and swallowed before she began.

"My father has a drinking and gambling problem," she spilled. "And I mean, a real problem. It has cost us so much, money and… other things. He lost his car, our home, and his business. My mother tried to make everything work out but we couldn't afford London prices and when we lost the house… we were on the streets for a couple months until my best friend from school, your cousin's friend, Geoffrey Ainsley, Marquess of Garvey, heir to the dukedom of Torrington, took my family in to stay at his townhouse. My mother had gotten sick while we lived on the streets and slowly, she deteriorated. Geoff got the best doctors, but nothing helped. She died soon after. My father worked through his grief by going to meetings for gamblers and alcoholics. He was doing well. He got a job and we were able to move into a little place on our own in Bromley. It was wonderful for a time. Dad really tried.

"But on the first-year anniversary of mum's death, he hadn't gotten home before me which was unusual and when I called, he didn't answer. He came home early that next morning, stumbling around, missing the timepiece I had bought him, and his pocketbook. I realized what happened. When he sobered up, he apologized over and over again, promising he would never touch another drop nor gamble, ever again. He kept that promise until the next year's anniversary and the next and the next," she looked down. "Finally, two days ago he came home, again on the anniversary, and told me…" Frustrated with the tears that started when she spoke about her mother, she swiped at her cheeks. Clearing her throat, she continued. "He told me, he had been at the table with several others but most notably, Anthony Rossi. I had met him once at a gala for the Humane Society at which I volunteer. Apparently, my dad lost a lot of money… money we didn't have. Anthony made him a deal. One more hand of cards and Anthony would wager all the money dad owed if he would give me over to him for a five-year trial marriage. Dad lost."

Corinne saw Lachlan's eyes widen and his hands clenched around the mug of coffee.

"I ran. Geoff helped me and here I am."

They were quiet for a long moment. "So," Lachlan finally said, his voice rough. "Your father sold you to that bastard expecting you to have no say in this? And if you refuse, he'll take you with or without your consent."

She nodded. "That's why I left."

"And rightly so," he growled. "What the hell was he thinking?"

"I don't think he was," she admitted. "He was drunk and thought he could win."

"Well, he didn't," Lachlan shook his head. "And you have to deal with the fallout. Thank God you got away."

"But I can't stay," she said.

"Why not?"

"Because I'm certain he'll find me, and he'll hurt anyone in his way... Anyone." She looked at him pointedly.

"I can handle a wee bastard like him."

"You don't understand. I could never be the cause of you being hurt. I hardly know you, but I couldn't let anyone be hurt."

Lachlan set his mug of coffee aside, leaned forward, and took her hand in his. "I know we've only just met this evening, but I can tell you would never want anyone to get hurt and you'd rather go on your own than to have anyone help you. I respect that, trust me. But, Corinne, you have to let people help you sometimes and fighting a mobster in a foreign country is one of those times."

Lightning struck and thunder boomed outside. Corinne screeched. Only then did she realize how quiet it had been. The surge of fear and adrenaline raced through her and she didn't know if she wanted to weep or fight."

Lachlan crouched down in front of her. "You're safe here," he said softly.

"But you're not."

"I will be fine, I promise you that. You have enough to worry about."

The corner of his lip ticked up and she couldn't stop herself. She leaned forward, ran her fingers through his hair, and slid down off the chair to kneel with him.

His eyes questioned but he didn't try to stop her. She wondered what his kiss might be like. She may never have had sex, but she still had plenty of experience kissing and she was certain Lachlan would be an excellent kisser.

Curiosity, fear, adrenaline all culminated at once as she leaned forward to close the distance between them.

Too many things were running through Lachlan's mind to think about the subtle change behind Corinne's eyes. But when she ran her fingers through his hair, goosebumps rose on his arms and scalp. When she knelt before him, he knew he should never allow it to go further but part of him was too fascinated to stop. And the other part missed a woman's touch. The second he felt her warm breath on his lips, his wife's battered and bloody face flashed before his eyes.

With the cry of anguish, he pulled back and gently pushed against her shoulders, parting their bodies before their lips met. Corinne gasped and instantly her cheeks turned pink.

"I'm sorry," she breathed.

He shook his head and closed his eyes. "No," he answered. "*I'm* sorry. I can't."

"I understand. Forgive me. Thank you. I was feeling vulnerable and I nearly took advantage of you. I am mortified," she said.

"It's fine. Really," he assured, but in his gut, he knew it wasn't. He wanted her. He had to fight it. Blaming the proximity, the storm, and the heightened emotions, he slowly got to his feet and offered his hand to her. Once she was up right, he did not let go of her hand and let his thumbs stroke her knuckles.

"Corinne, it's not… I do feel something when we're together but…"

"You don't have to explain anything, Lachlan," she said. "I do understand. Thank you and I'm sorry I pressured you."

"You didn't. The storm should be ending soon. That was the eye that just passed through, hence the quiet. I'm not tired," Lachlan admitted. He was too wired to sleep. "Go ahead and get some rest. I'll stay with Oscar."

"Are you sure?"

"Yes," he answered. "The worst is over for him. He won't need much more monitoring."

"All right, thank you… for everything."

"My pleasure," he replied then realizing how his words could be interpreted, went on. "I mean, it's fine. Not to worry."

Lachlan watched as Corinne headed back to his room. As soon as she turned the corner, he let out the breath he had been holding and fell back in the chair. He needed to make it through the rest of their time together without an incident. He wasn't sure how he was he going to fight the attraction between them.

He never believed in instant feelings. Instalove stories his late wife used to read, or the kind of *love at first sight* his grandfather and Uncle Emmet had experienced, but he didn't know what else to call it. He didn't remember when he first met Karin, they had known each other in Primary School for years before he grew interested. He cared for Corinne almost instantly and he'd be damned if he let some slimy, smarmy, bastard take her away against her will.

He'd protect her. *But how?* He wondered.

Chapter Eleven

Lachlan slowly woke to the smell of frying bacon, fresh coffee, scones, and eggs. He took a deep breath before he opened his eyes. It had been years since he had woken to those smells and all at once, the events from the night before, came back to him. His eyes shot open and he looked toward the kitchen, glancing at the table where Oscar had slept. The dog was sitting at the entrance of the kitchen watching the activity inside.

Clearing his throat gently to rid it of the early morning frog that had taken residence, he stood and check the time on his phone. There was still no service, but the sun was playing between the clouds. When eight fifteen showed on the screen, he blinked in surprise, followed immediately by guilt. He had fallen asleep at his post. Happy with Oscar's recovery, he remembered pouring himself a small glass of whiskey around three in the morning and drinking it down. After Corinne had left, he couldn't get his wife's face out of his mind and one time, just before the whiskey, Karin's face changed to Corinne's and it was her body on the gurney; battered, bloody, dead

Glancing around the room, extra candles had been lit and someone had covered him with a blanket which lay at the foot of the chair. Grabbing it, he folded the woolen throw and set it over the back of the chair.

"Good morning," Corinne's voice came from behind him and as with the night before every hair on his arms and neck stood on end.

Slowly, he turned to her and the smile that lifted his lips was genuine. Her hair was pulled up into a ponytail, something he always enjoyed because it gave him free reign to his woman's neck... and she was barefoot, her pink toenails peeking out from beneath the legs of his oversized sweatpants. Looking up, he saw her bright eyes watching him in the tinge of pink in her cheeks. She looked away and bit her lower lip, a move that had his own lips tingling.

He shook his head. *What is wrong with me?* He had spent the last ten years happily celibate, not so much as a stirring for another woman and there he was, practically undressing the woman he promised to protect. He was sick. That was all there was to it. Sick in the head.

"I hope you don't mind. I made breakfast," she said indicating the tray.

"Not at all," he answered. "You must have figured out how to work the cooker."

She shrugged and set the tray down on the eating table,

the one Oscar had lain on. It was clean and Lachlan caught a faint smell of ammonia.

"Living on the streets, you learn how to cook on anything."

He paused. Her confessions from the night before still fresh on both their minds. Oscar padded over to Lachlan and instinctually, Lachlan crouched down and checked the hound.

"Hiya, lad," he said. "How do you feel? Better?"

Oscar whimpered but licked his chin. Lachlan grinned at the dog. "You're welcome, lad," he said. "Glad I could help."

"I changed the dressing this morning. Your stitches held and no inflammation," Corinne said.

"Good, that's good," he replied. Standing, he walked over to her. "Thank you for the blanket. I don't remember falling asleep."

"It's all right. I got up around five, unable to sleep anymore. When I came out here looking for some water, I saw you were asleep, and Oscar was just waking up."

"Breakfast smells wonderful," he said.

"I saw you enjoyed hot sauce. I found some peppers and used them in the eggs but if you'd like some, I brought it out."

Lachlan flinched at the pain in his chest. Not since Karin had anyone paid attention to what he liked.

"My late wife was obsessed with it," he explained. "She introduced it to me."

"I've never had it."

"Have some with me?" he offered. She grinned and nodded. As they sat at the table, they talked about Ireland, County Kerry specifically. Lachlan admitted he had moved to Dublin for nine years and only just moved back about three months ago.

They had just finished when Lachlan's phone rang multiple notifications all at once and Corinne's rang four times.

"Service is back," Lachlan explained as he stood and grabbed both of their phones. Corinne gasped in relief when she saw the texts.

"Geoffrey is worried, I'm going to call him."

"Feel free to use my room."

"Thanks," she stood and walked over to the bedroom, dialing her best friend as Lachlan checked his messages.

Two were from his father letting him know service had cut out but hoped one of his text might get through. There was a downed tree at the base of the road cutting off his route to the office.

Four from his mother hoping he was all right and wishing he had stayed over.

One from one of the farmers in the area, letting him know that his lambs began giving birth and if he was able, could he come check on the mommas.

He sent a text to the farmer letting him know he would be over as soon as he could and then dialed his mother.

"Oh, thank God, honey, are you all right?" His mother asked as soon as she answered.

"Heya, Ma, yeah, I'm fine," he replied. "The storm rattled some windows but it's not terrible. How did you fair?"

"We lost power around ten, but I had gotten enough nonperishable food. A few tree limbs down but not as bad as further up the coast. Some places are flooded. So, it could have been worse but we're all right. Still no power though phones are back which is a relief. How are you doing on food and water?"

"We're fine, Ma, thanks to you."

She paused. "We?" She questioned.

Shite. "Uh, yeah," he replied. "I had a visitor in need of medical assistance late last night. Her dog was injured."

"Her?"

Shite, again.

"Yes, Corinne. She's checking in at home and as soon as the main roads are clear, she and her dog will be on their way…"

Not if he had anything to say about it, but he didn't need his mother getting ideas. It was hard enough ignoring how he was beginning to feel about her.

"Oh, well good, honey." Surprisingly, his mother let it drop. "The weatherman says the worst is over and we should have good weather later. Maybe you and… Corinne could come over for dinner?"

"Will see, Ma," he replied. "Did Oisín get back home before it started raining?"

"He got a little wet, but he's fine, love."

"Good. Could you let da' know I got his message about the downed tree?"

"I will, sweetheart. When will we see you?"

"Soon, Ma. We'll see about dinner or maybe lunch on her way out tomorrow."

"She's staying another night?"

"Yeah," he revealed. "Don't get any ideas, Ma. I'm sleeping

in the chair."

"Honey," she scolded. "I would never think that you would presume such a thing. You are a gentleman. But, if it were to happen, we would understand and be happy for you."

"Not going there with you, Ma."

"I just mean that sex is part of life. Your father and I were still highly active at your age. Even now."

"Ma, please, I'm begging you… stop."

"All I mean, darling is we understand and so would Karin. You've mourned her for over ten years. She would want you to live a little."

And there it was, the anger and pain and the walls around his heart went right back up. The bricks still strong though slightly cracked.

"Ma, it's not going to happen. Thank you for your call, I will let you know what I decide."

"Now, just wait one more minute, young man. You do not cut your mother off like that. I know I overstepped and I'm sorry. I promised you I wouldn't. I just got a little excited for you… You know, I heard somewhere a mother is only as happy as her least happy child. I believe that. Now, I will let you go. I'm sorry. I love you and you don't have to worry about me saying anything like that again."

Great, now I felt like an arse.

Sighing harshly, he looked back toward the bedroom door. Corinne had helped him. She broke down some barriers around his heart and mind. She showed him it would help to let someone in so he didn't fight alone. He had someone on the other end of the phone who fit the criteria. Someone who loved him unconditionally, and who would never judge him.

"I'm sorry, Ma," he said. "The truth is... I..."

"What, love?" She asked softly.

"You remember grandda's *lightning* talk about gramma?"

"Yes, of course, he always talked about it."

"Yeah, I – ehm, know what he means, now."

"You mean?"

"Lightning. And it's damn hard not to embrace it. But I keep seeing Karin's face... I don't know what to do."

His mother was quiet for a long moment, so long he had to check the connection twice.

"Finally," she spoke softly. "Lach, what's really holding you back? We all loved Karin and we all know what she would say. She never would have wanted you to pine for her. Son, you're thirty-eight years old... you have your whole life ahead of you. Can you honestly tell me that she would want you like this?"

"No," he said softly, his voice cracking.

"Then what is holding you back?"

This is it. His last confession.

"I didn't save her, Ma," he said. "I couldn't, she begged me to save our daughter and I couldn't. She begged me... as she was dying... to save her but I couldn't. I couldn't. I..." his throat constricted, and tears ran down his cheeks. His legs gave out, but two arms caught him. He looked over and saw Corinne's face beside him. He held her gaze as if it gave him strength. "I couldn't save her, and she knew it. She died knowing I failed her. I failed the two people I loved more than anything on earth."

"Shh," Corinne stroked the back of his hair.

"Oh, sweetheart," he heard his mother's tears through the speaker. "You loved Karin and Hope so much, she knows... she *knew* how much you loved them. My dearest boy, don't punish yourself any longer. It was an accident, a horrible, senseless accident and it stole two beautiful, wonderful lives... Don't let it steal another."

With his mother's words in one ear and Corinne's soothing hums in the other, something broke inside him. The pain, the heartache, the anger, was released and just as quickly as the tears began, they ended. He held his mobile to his ear and Corinne held him, Oscar in front of him, his head laying in his lap.

"You have to start living again."

Those were words to live by. Could he though? Could he put all the emotions from the past decade away and could he let anyone in without worrying they would be stolen from him too?

He looked over at Corinne, tears in her eyes for him. "Thank you..." he said into the phone and not dropping Corinne's gaze.

"I love you, honey. I know she's there now, so I'll sign off. Call me. I'm always here."

He didn't hear his mother say goodbye as he stared into the watery depths of Corinne's blue eyes. But he lowered the phone to the floor and turned to face Corinne. He placed one hand around the back of her head, his fingers tangling in her hair and pulled her to him.

Their lips connected and he groaned at the sweet feeling flooding his veins. It had been far too long since he felt a connection with a woman. The silky feel of her lips on his, the tentative movements of a couple's first kiss, slowly burned into a deeper flame. Corinne's tongue teased his lower lip and he opened easily for her. Their tongues battled with each other and her nails raked the shorter hair at the back of his head. He groaned and she quickly pulled back.

"Did I hurt you?" She questioned.

Oh, she is beyond adorable.

"No," he breathed. "Not at all."

"Oh, good. I… wasn't sure."

"You never heard a man groan in ecstasy before?" He chuckled but her pink cheeks and darting glance sent red flags straight to his brain. "Corinne?"

She peeked up at him, an innocence in her face. He couldn't be right, there was no way, not how she kissed but… there it was.

"Corinne… are you a virgin?"

She took a shuddery breath. "Yes," she finally answered and his whole world turned upside down.

Chapter Twelve

Corinne could hear Lachlan on the phone with his mother as she waited in his room for Geoffrey to answer her call.

"I have been worried sick," he finally said. "Are you okay?"

"Sorry, yes. I lost service just as I pulled into Killarney. It's a long story but I'm fine."

"Oh, thank God," he breathed. "What happened? Did you find the hostel?"

Corinne sighed and launched into the story of the past twenty-four hours.

Geoffrey listened quietly until she was finished.

"Honey," he said. "I've only met Lachlan once, are you sure you can trust him? I mean you hardly know him."

"I have a good feeling about him."

Geoffrey was quiet again. "I'll call Peter. He knows him better. Sit tight until I call back."

"I know he's fine, okay. You don't have to do that."

"I know, I don't have to, babe... look, I'm not saying I don't trust him just promise you'll be careful. I love you and can't get to you if you need me." The memory of Geoff fighting one of Rossi's men in her dream came back to her and she shivered.

"I love you too," she answered. "And I'm okay really... I really like him."

"Like, *like* him, like him?"

"Very mature, Marquess."

"Don't roll your eyes, honey. I'm serious. You've liked a lot of guys in the past."

"You're one to talk."

"We're not talking about me. But all I'm saying is, you're frightened about Rossi and this guy basically showed up like a knight in shining armor. I just want to make sure he's... you know, legit and you realize he's still just a guy and I don't want you falling for him without really knowing him. And no, I don't know him well enough to make a judgement call. Last I met him was five years ago and he hardly spoke. I worry about you, Corrie, that's all. I wouldn't be your best friend I didn't."

"I know. Just trust me, Geoff, I have a good feeling about him. If it would make you feel better, call Peter and check on him."

"Okay, I trust you, honey. I told you to trust your gut and if your gut is telling you to go after this guy, then do it."

She said nothing but sighed in relief. "Have you heard anything from your dad?"

"Nothing yet," he admitted. "I'll call him again and see."

"Thank you, Geoff. For everything."

"Hey, I love you, babe. You know I do anything for you. But now, let's get off the phone. I don't want to run the risk of anyone listening in."

"Okay, I'll text you later?"

"Please do, so I know you're safe. I'll call Peter."

They hung up after a *goodbye* and *talk soon* and Corinne immediately heard a cry and sniffles coming from the living room. She hurried to the door to see Lachlan on the phone, tears in his eyes, repeating the words *I couldn't save her*. Corinne rushed to him as his knees gave out. He was talking about his wife. She was sure of it. He had told her Karin had been pregnant when she died. Corinne couldn't fathom the pain he was going through. After his mother calmed him a bit, he hung up the phone and the look in his eyes told her everything she needed to know.

As she expected, Lachlan knew how to kiss. Her toes curled on the hardwood floors. But when he groaned, she thought she had hurt him, maybe her nail had snagged on his scalp. Little did she realize; she would have to answer the one question she never wanted to answer. Geoff was the only one who knew. Her own father didn't know she was a virgin but when Lachlan asked, she had to tell him the truth. Somehow knowing he would not make fun of her, she looked up at him, sighed, and finally answered.

"Yes."

Chapter Thirteen

Indianapolis, Indiana

"Babe, what do you think about this one?" Vivian called to her fiancé. Peter Carlisle walked over to see what she was pointing to and held in his grimace.

"It's a little…"

"Extra?" Vivian questioned, her face falling in disappointment.

They had been looking for a new living room set for their new house just north of downtown Indianapolis. Peter didn't consider himself a picky person, but some of Vivian's choices were… a bit much. He enjoyed tasteful and modest, Vivian was into more nineteen-sixties with bright colors and vintage patterns.

Sometimes he missed the military. Shared barracks with fifty other guys and having a colorful palette of... dark greens and muted browns to choose from. Geoff always made light of it and Peter wished his best friend was there now.

"Earth to Peter," Vivian's voice shook him from his thoughts.

"Sorry, babe," he replied. "What?"

"Look, I know it's frustrating. I know my tastes don't *exactly* match up with yours but... it would help, if you were into this, you know?"

"I know," he heaved a sigh. "It's just, we need space for our family and yet, I wanna make sure you get everything you want but nothing here is really catching my eye. I'm sorry."

She smiled sweetly. "Have I told you today how amazing you are?" Vivian asked sliding her hands up Peter's arms to his shoulders.

"Not that I remember," Peter smirked.

"Well, you are and the sooner we can pick out a sofa, the faster we can get home and I can prove it to you."

"I like the sound of that," Peter leaned down but pulled away when his phone rang a ringtone he hadn't heard in a little while.

"Saved by the bell," Vivian breathlessly said.

"It's Geoff," Peter explained and saw the cloud of jealousy descend on his fiancée's face, but it vanished before Peter could say anything.

"Well, what are you waiting for? His Highness awaits," she replied. "I'll keep looking."

Peter nodded. He knew why Vivian was a little jealous. He and Geoff had always been closer than brothers. They met in Afghanistan, but Peter could only remember parts of their initial meeting. After losing his squadron in the desert, he was captured by Al Qaeda forces. A POW for months. When he woke in the military hospital in Germany, Geoff, his savior was right next to him. Since then, they became best friends.

He watched Vivian walk down the aisle looking at and testing couches, deliberately not looking in his direction. Huffing a sigh, Peter accepted the call.

"Lord Garvey," he teased. Geoff chuckled.

"Carlisle." *Damn*, his voice still raised the hair in his arms. "Did I catch it a good time?"

"Yeah, Viv and I are out shopping for the house."

"Oh right," he hesitated. "I'm glad things are going well for you both."

And there it is. Geoff could never express his true emotions. He claimed it was the English aristocracy in him. But Peter knew Geoff did not like Vivian, and Peter didn't know why.

"So, what's up? Or did you call just to say hello?" Peter asked.

"As much as I wish, no. Do you remember my friend Corinne McDonnagh?"

"The girl you set up at the townhouse a few years ago?"

"The same," Geoffrey said.

"I remember, why?"

"Here's the thing," Geoff began. "She's in danger and I helped her get to Ireland. I remembered you had family over there."

"Yeah, the O'Quinn's," Peter caught Vivian's glance and forced a smile.

"Corrie met someone who says he's part of the O'Quinns and I remember meeting him but only once. I wanted to check in. It's Lachlan."

"Lach, yeah," Peter answered. "Well, as you know he's Trevor's cousin, the eldest cousin."

"I never got to know him well. What can you tell me about him?" Geoff asked.

"Well, he's a veterinarian and a widower. His wife was hit by a teenager and was pregnant with his daughter at the time. Trevor said it was a horrible time for the family. Whenever I'm around, he's nice. A bit jaded and secluded but he is a great guy. They all are. Like something out of the nineteen forties without the whole degrading women thing."

"So, he would be a good man for a friend?" Geoff asked.

Peter's brows shot up. "Well, I mean, I guess. He'll be some work though. He's still not over his wife's death."

Geoff was quiet on the other end.

"What's really going on, Geoff?" Peter asked.

"It's nothing. Don't worry about it," Geoff said.

"It's not nothing. You said she was in danger. Are you in danger too?" Peter questioned.

"I'm fine," Geoff assured.

"Promise?"

"Yes, I gotta go."

"Please text me later, so I know you're all right," Peter was dangerously close to crossing a line, a line they agreed existed for a reason.

"I will. I'll be fine, don't worry."

"I'll always worry about you."

That line vanished as he crossed it so fast it was left in the dust.

"Just stop, Peter, all right? We agreed. We're not... in Germany anymore. You wanted space and... Vivian. I appreciate your concern, but you need to stop." he paused. Then without preamble, spoke again. "I have to go."

Peter bit his tongue when he heard the beep indicating he hung up. Gripping the phone seeing the black screen, Peter took a deep breath and let it out slowly. Ever since Vivian, Peter's and Geoff's relationship grew strained.

Looking for Vivian, he didn't see her immediately. He found her sitting in the outdoor furniture section on a bench swing, her gaze on nothing in particular, a faraway look in her eyes. Their new home had only a concrete slab for a back patio and Peter had promised he would put in a proper space for her as Vivian loved to entertain. But it was the look on her face that worried him. Vivian looked so empty.

"Find a set you liked?" He tried to lift the mood. Vivian glanced up at him, then looked away.

Peter took a seat next to her. Vivian stood and walked over to the umbrellas, standing a few feet away. Peter sighed, stood, and wiped his suddenly sweaty hands on his jeans.

Walking up behind her, he placed his hands on Vivian's upper arms which she promptly shook off.

"Viv," Peter questioned. "What's wrong?"

Vivian said nothing and moved to the rugs near the umbrellas.

"Vivian."

She huffed a sigh and turned to Peter. "What?"

"What's wrong?"

"What's wrong?" Vivian questioned. "I don't know, Peter, maybe it's the fact that my fiancé and I can't decide on a sofa because our tastes are so different. Or maybe, it's because every damn time Geoff calls, I'm clearly forgotten. I think you need to ask yourself, are you one hundred percent committed to us or are you... do you want him? Because every time he calls, you act like a lovesick puppy and completely change from the man I love. If you're not sure about this, I need to know now. I can't keep acting like this doesn't bother me."

"I thought you liked Geoffrey. We've stayed at his house a few times when we travel."

"Yeah, and you wanna know how much sleep I get when we stay over? None. I'm far too concerned you'll slip away and go to him. I'm tired of worrying I'm not enough for you. So just tell me, were you two... together? Are you bi?"

"That sounds more like an issue with you than with me."

"Oh, you do, do you? Am I the one who didn't answer the question? Am I the one who has a stupid grin on my face whenever he calls? Am I the one who secretly texts him when I think you're asleep? Oh yeah, I know for a fact you do that. So no, buddy boy, it's not me who has the insecurity problem. You need to think long and hard about this. If you aren't sure, even a little bit, tell me now."

Peter knew she was right, and it hurt him to know that was

how Vivian felt. Yes, he and Geoffrey had history, war would do that. But Vivian was his future. And no matter how tough it was for Geoffrey and him, he would always be fond of him, but he loved Vivian.

"I love you," Peter said. "I love how easy it is with you, how amazing you are. How you care about everyone and no one is a stranger. I love how you aren't afraid to be yourself with everyone and how you don't care about anyone's opinion because you're not doing it for them but for yourself. And most of all, I love how you love me. So, I am one hundred percent committed to us, to you, to this, Vivian. I love you and though I have a friend who I care about, there is nothing between us. I want you and you alone." Vivian had not dropped his gaze while he spoke. He pulled her closer. "And if you want that yellow couch, then dammit, get that yellow couch."

Vivian grinned at his words. "No taksies backsies."

Peter groaned. "Just please no egg chairs."

"No fair!" Vivian laughed. She grew serious and rested her head on Peter's chest. "I want to be enough for you, Pete. I don't want to lose you and yeah, I'm a bit territorial. Sue me. You're my man. You best remember it. I won't be so nice next time."

"That was you being nice?" Peter teased.

"Yes, don't make mama bear come out of hibernation," Vivian winked.

"I kinda like it when you growl."

Vivian laughed. "Down boy."

Peter beamed and was grateful to have her back, even if it was because of a white lie. His reactions to Geoffrey always were confusing to him. He didn't understand it. But he did not *love* him, *do I?* he wondered as he took her hand and forced a smile.

Chapter Fourteen

Lachlan stared at Corinne. Part of him was stunned, the other part was proud of her. He had only ever known one woman in his life and they had been each other's firsts on their wedding night.

"Is it an issue?" She questioned.

"Issue?"

"I've been told I don't kiss badly. In fact, my ex-boyfriend told me he rather liked the way I kissed."

"No, no, it's not a problem at all." *It just tells me to cool off,* he thought. He wiped his face and stood slowly, his legs still shaky from all the emotion.

"Lachlan?" She asked, standing too. "Please don't let this change anything. I may not know what to do, but I'm a quick learner."

He started. That was as blatant as any invitation he had ever received.

"Corinne, I'm not going to sleep with you."

"Why not?" She crossed her arms over her chest.

"Because…" he said.

"Because why? I'm not good enough for you?"

Lachlan shook his head. "Stop. You are more mature than that."

She stared at him for a long moment. Finally, the fight in her dissipated. "You're right. I'm sorry. It's just I've waited for so long to give myself to someone I cared for and now it looks like my first time will not only be forced but by a man I hate."

His blood boiled. "You will *not* be giving yourself to that bastard. I don't care what he has over you. You are to be treasured and desired and loved. I will not let him touch you."

"You don't have a choice in the matter, Lachlan," she said. "I wanted to be with someone like you. Someone good, kind, and loving but, my father… He's chosen for me."

"That's not true," he said.

"Yes, it is, there's no way out of this for me."

"I'm not going to argue with you, all right. But the woman I met last night wouldn't give up so easily. Now, you're safe here, from Rossi and from me. I refuse to take advantage of you."

92

Corinne took a deep breath and walked over to him, taking his hands.

"I'm sorry. Thank you. I don't usually throw myself at anyone especially not an attractive man."

The corner of his lip ticked up. "You think I'm attractive, huh?" She bit her lower lip but nodded. "Thank you," he said. "And for the record, I find you very attractive as well."

She grinned but her cell phone rang, and she pulled it out. "It's Geoff. He called Peter to check up on you."

"What? Why?" He chuckled.

"He's worried about me."

"He sounds like a good friend. I'm sorry I didn't get a chance to get to know him better."

"He is," she agreed and answered the phone.

Lachlan didn't hear Geoff side of the conversation. He headed to the kitchen to wash the breakfast plates and coffee cups. His eyes glanced over to Oscar, who was resting in front of the wood burning fireplace. His eyebrows moved as he looked at both Corinne and Lachlan.

"I told you," he heard Corinne say. "I told you he was wonderful. Yes, I know. I'll be careful." There was a pause as she lowered her voice to a whisper. "Geoff, stop. I'm not going to do… that." Then, she giggled.

Lachlan chuckled. He was flattered she wanted to be with him. But there was no way he could take her up on the offer, no matter how she affected him. And for once it wasn't because of his late wife, it was because her admission showed him, she deserved to give herself to someone who loved her. She had waited for the right time and the right guy, just as he and Karin had waited. She deserved to feel exactly as they did. He dried his hands and looked out into the living room. She looked so young, he wondered for the first time how old she was and if he knew anyone her age he could trust. Never one to play matchmaker before, he knew she would be an amazing help mate for anyone. Her ability to help him heal was proof of that. Scars remained, but for the first time in ten years, he was able to breathe, laugh, and actually enjoy himself again without feeling guilty for it.

The thought of another by her side, made him pause.

"Are you all right?" Her voice came from the living room and he realized he was staring at her.

"Sorry, yes," he answered.

"Sorry about Geoff. You didn't... hear anything?"

He grinned. "Enough."

Her cheeks pinked and she looked away. "Sorry."

"Did he warn you not to sleep with me?"

She shook her head. "He encouraged it."

Lachlan laughed outright. "Well then, I have to thank him."

"Apparently, Peter sung your praises."

"Did he?" He raised an eyebrow. "He's a good man."

She shuffled from one foot to the other. This awkwardness wasn't her. Something was on her mind.

"Lachlan, I want to apologize. I can only imagine how it must look to you, throwing myself at you like that. I'm sorry."

"Don't think any more on it, okay? It's fine. And I don't think any less of you."

"Thank you for that," she said. They said nothing for a long moment then she glanced at the door. "Do you think we can get my bags? I would like to shower and change clothes. If that's all right."

"Of course," Lachlan said with a glance at the grey clouds. "It's only overcast. Let's go now before it rains again."

She nodded and watched as he grabbed her raincoat and offered it to her. He pulled on his Wellies and grabbed an umbrella. They told Oscar to stay and headed out.

Chapter Fifteen

Corinne and Lachlan walked together in silence. She was thankful for the time to think. She was so embarrassed. She had all but thrown herself into his arms. But the knowledge that Geoff's father hadn't had any new, scared her senseless. She knew it was only a matter of time until she was found. Her dream proved that, and that fact made her want to run and never look back but even in the short time she'd known Lachlan, she knew he was good and kind and everything she thought she wanted. He made her laugh, protected and challenged her, respected and helped her. If she wasn't absolutely certain they had only just met, she would swear, she'd known him her whole life.

As the last of the drizzling rain hit her face, she thanked

her lucky stars her car broke down so near his cottage. Seeing the little red car before her, she realized how stupid it was to drive such a small car in the middle of a hurricane.

Lachlan walked over to the driver's side and opened the door. In her haste, she hadn't locked the doors. Thankful her things hadn't been stolen, she watched as he popped the hood and took a look at the engine.

"There's a few things I see that may have caused it, but I'll call my cousin, Killian. He works with his uncle at the garage." He pulled out his phone.

"You know everyone, don't you?"

He shrugged. "We O'Quinns are a large family and we're all pretty close." She waited as he dialed. "Kill, it's Lach, hey listen, are you and Uncle Tom swamped after the storm? Good, I have a job for you." He launched into the story about her car and what happened, leaving out any embarrassing details. "I'm here at the car now to get her things, do you think you could come and take a look? I know the main roads are still blocked... Cheers, Kill, thanks." He gave him the location and hung up, looking over at Corinne, he smiled. "He can't get the tow out until the roads are clear but he's going to walk over from his parent's house and take a look to see if it's something he can fix without the shop."

"That would be wonderful."

"But the main roads will not be clear until at least tomorrow. If he can fix it, you can drive it over to my place and leave it there."

"Oh, I couldn't impose."

"Not an imposition," he promised. "You're welcome to stay over too, for as long as you need."

She thought for a long moment. Immediately, she wanted

to say both yes and no. Yes, because she wanted to stay with him, be around him. No, because she had already made a fool of herself and couldn't trust herself around him. But it would be best for Oscar.

"Maybe for only another day or so."

"However long," he stressed.

"Thank you."

They stayed silent for another minute until Lachlan spoke. "If you want to go back to the cottage, I'll wait here for my cousin and bring your bags."

"I don't mind. After being cooped up, it's nice to get out."

Lachlan agreed and stuffed his hands into his jeans pocket.

"My ma has invited us to dinner if you want. I can show you the village and introduce you to Mrs. Jacobson."

"I'd like that."

"Something other than my cooking," he chuckled.

"I liked your cooking," she admitted.

"I'm glad, I'll have to make you something more than BLTs."

"That sounds good." Again, they were quiet. "Thank you," she finally blurted.

He turned to her. "For what?"

"For everything."

His lips tipped up. "You're welcome."

Again, they waited. She didn't like the awkward silence between them. After their kiss and her subsequent admittance, he had withdrawn.

"Lachlan," she said softly. He looked down at her. "I hope my... I hope what we talked about and did hasn't changed anything between us. I want you to know I appreciate everything you've done for Oscar and me. I enjoy talking to you."

"I enjoy talking with you too, Corinne. And no, it doesn't change anything. I've gone through a lot today and I'm sorry I'm a bit reserved. But no, nothing has changed between us."

She beamed. She could understand that and was glad.

"Lach!" They heard his cousin call. Turning they saw the twenty-one-year-old taking big steps up the side of the steep hill, a smile on his lips. Lachlan greeted his cousin with a warm embrace.

Chapter Sixteen

Lachlan was glad for the distraction. His mind was all over the place. After everything that happened in his cottage earlier that day, he wasn't sure which way was up anymore. He was holding himself together by a thread. It was good to see his cousin. Family always grounded him. Killian was second born to Lachlan's Uncle Emmet and Aunt Mara. Killian and his twin sister Aiofe were like night and day in everything but looks. Though, physically impossible to be identical twins, there was no question they were related. Killian and Aiofe looked just like their mother Mara but one thing they did have that was undeniably from their father, where their ice blue eyes. Emmet had the bluest eyes and he passed that trait on to all three of his children; Trevor, Killian, and Aiofe.

Killian and Lachlan clapped hands and pulled each other into a backslapping hug

"Good to see you home. Sorry I haven't been by, it's been crazy at the garage," Killian said.

Three years ago, Killian announced he wasn't going to a traditional four-year college. Instead, he was going to study mechanics to help his Uncle Tom in the dealer shop Emmet used to own.

Since then, he had advanced to shop manager and would soon be part owner with their aunts' husbands, Tom and Paddy.

"No worries," Lachlan replied. "Thanks for coming out. How did Uncle Emmet and Aunt Mara fair during the storm?"

"No damages to the house, but I'm scarred for life. They found ways to conserve body heat and forgot to lock the door," Killian chuckled.

"I've been there, mate," Lachlan grinned. "It's never a good thing for us. No kid should see their parents like that."

Killian fake shivered in disgust. Lachlan laughed and Killian stared. "I think that's the first time I've ever heard you laugh."

Lachlan sobered, squeezed his cousin's shoulder, and turned to Corinne. "Kill, this is Corinne. It was her car that broke down yesterday during the storm."

"Nice to meet you," Corinne said.

"Likewise," Killian smiled, but Lachlan was glad to see it wasn't a flirtatious smile.

"Let me take a look. Can you describe what happened?" He

stepped toward the open hood of the car.

"I was letting my dog out before the storm got too bad and when I got back inside, the key turned but there was no sound. Nothing happened."

Killian nodded and checked a couple things inside the engine block then went to the driver side. Lachlan tossed him the keys he had grabbed from the ignition when he had tried to start it, and Killian folded his five-foot eleven-inch frame into the seat.

Killian tried to turn the key a couple times; his ear cocked to listen for something. When clearly nothing happened, he got out and checked a couple more things, then shook his head. "Well, good news is you were close enough to my cousin's place to wait out the storm. Bad news is the battery is dead."

"Can you charge it?" Lachlan asked.

"Not without a jump and even then, it doesn't look good. Is this your car?" Killian asked her.

"No," Corinne shook her head. "It's a rental."

"Well, get your money back. The battery is pretty corroded," he shook his head. "They should never have let you drive it."

"Can you tow it once the roads are clear?" Lachlan asked.

"Definitely, but they're saying it's going to be at least a couple more days. The lads are down there now removing the sandbags they created for the break wall. They won't get much more than that done today."

"Do you want to leave it here?" Lachlan looked over at her. "We could push it back to my place."

"Not likely," Killian stated. "There's too much rocky terrain. There's no easy way."

"We could try," Lachlan replied.

"My professional recommendation would be to leave it here until I can get the tow. It may seem silly, but it won't be easy pushing it. At least not without Oisín," Killian said. "Besides, let me document it where it is, it will give you more clout with the rental company. If we try to push it and something happens to the car, they can hold you responsible."

"Yeah, let's not do that. They gave me a faulty car, it serves them right if I leave it here for a couple days," Corinne said.

Killian grinned. "I like her, Lach, even if she is English." He winked.

Lachlan bit his tongue on the words he almost said. *I like her too.*

Killian locked up the car and toss the keys to Lachlan.

"Well, I'll see you guys later. Let's get a pint sometime, aye?"

"Sure thing," Lachlan clasped his cousin's hand and hugged him. Even with almost twenty years age difference between the two men, Lachlan always tried to treat his younger cousins as cousins and not children even if he used to mind them when their parents asked. That was the joy of having a close family, sitters on demand.

Corinne and Lachlan watched as Killian walked down the hill toward the village.

"He seems nice," Corinne said.

"He is and very hardworking which is something not everyone in his generation understands."

"Okay, grandfather," Corinne grinned.

Lachlan chuckled. He was beginning to sound like his cousin, Egan.

"He seems pretty young. How old is he?"

"Twenty-one."

"I was similar at twenty-one. That was before my dad lost everything and I was at Uni."

Lachlan looked over at her. "Can I ask... How old are you?"

"Twenty-eight," she answered.

"My cousin Trevor's age," he breathed a sigh of relief. She was only ten years younger. He was worried she was younger still.

"Trevor... O'Quinn? The Broadway and opera star?" She asked.

"He is, yeah, you know him?"

"Geoff loves opera and has taken me to see him at the West End. He introduced us. Trevor was in a musical, it was around Christmas time."

"Yeah, *Pirates of Penzance*. He was excellent in that. He's my da's brother's son."

"Isn't he married?"

"Yes, to Cassandra Doyle-O'Quinn. They went to school together."

"Oh, she is wonderful too. I saw her as Fantine in *Les Miz*."

"She is. They've been married for nearly five years."

"Amazing... now, how old you are?"

"Promise you won't run away screaming?"

She giggled. "Don't know if you realize it but my car is not working and I don't know where I would go if I did, so you're stuck with me."

"I'm thirty-eight."

"That's all? Seriously, the way you were speaking I thought you were at least thirty-nine." She winked.

Lachlan chuckled. "All right, all right. Still…"

"Still what? You are very handsome man; any woman would be fortunate to be with you. And trust me, I've seen all of you."

Lachlan stared at her for a long moment. Then, he breathed a laugh. "Thanks for making it awkward."

"You're welcome."

"Now," he turned and grabbed the military green duffel bag from the trunk of the car. "Let's get back to Oscar. I want to check on him. You take your shower. Then, we will see what we can do about lunch." They started walking back toward his cottage.

"Do you want to go to your parent's house for dinner?"

"Do you? They want to meet you."

"I wouldn't mind," she answered.

"Then, I'll let them know. I do feel like I should warn you about my family. They are… a bit much."

"What do you mean?" She asked.

"They mean well, don't get me wrong. But they don't always say the right thing and some things they say, can be taken either way. But I can assure you, they never mean it in a negative way, at least… The only time I've seen it happen, was when one of my sister's ex-boyfriends showed up. Ma let him have it and not in a good way. He hightailed it out of there."

"I'm pretty sure that's allowed. I would probably have done the same."

"We all would. But just understand, they are an acquired taste."

"Lachlan, I'll be fine. Thank you, though."

"Good," they reached his cottage and he let her in. Oscar looked up from where he lay in front of the dying embers of the fireplace.

"Comfy, Oscar?" Corinne cooed.

Oscars tail began wagging slowly as Lachlan set her duffel on the chair and headed to the fireplace. Stoking the embers, he put more wood on the fire.

"You go ahead and take a shower. I'm gonna check on him and then run to one of the farms. Their ewes just began lambing," Lachlan explained from his crouched position by the fire.

"That's fine," she replied.

"You are welcome to any of the food if you get hungry. I'm not sure how long I'll be. I don't have a tele, I'm sorry. But my book selection is larger than most."

"Lachlan," she stopped him. "I'll be fine. Just let me know when you leave?"

"I will. And I'll take your bag to the bedroom."

"Thank you," she smiled and headed down the hallway to the bathroom. After Lachlan dropped off her duffel, he pulled out his phone. Sending a text to his mother letting her know they will be at dinner; he turned his attention to Oscar.

Chapter Seventeen

Lachlan returned to his cottage after checking in with the sheep farmer who had texted him during the hurricane and found Corinne sitting in his armchair, the fireplace roaring, and Oscar at her feet asleep. She looked up and smiled.

"How are the lambs?"

"Healthy," he replied.

"And the mommas?"

"He lost one, but the others are doing well," Lachlan admitted, shrugging out of his coat.

"As bad as it is losing one, at least it wasn't more."

"True," Lachlan replied. "I let Ma know we're coming to dinner. She's excited."

Corinne watched him and her gaze unnerved him.

"Why do I get the impression you don't want to go?"

He turned away.

"Lachlan? We don't have to if you don't want to." She stood and walked over to him.

"No, it's fine. It's just…"

"What?"

"They live near the church and at the church is—"

"The cemetery." She stated. Lachlan nodded. "Have you been since you've been back?" Lachlan shook his head. "I'll go with you," she offered. "You know, moral support?"

Lachlan looked up at her and held her gaze.

"I don't think I'm strong enough."

"You are," she took his hands in hers. "But you have to believe in yourself. It doesn't help if one thousand people believe in you. If you don't, it's not going to matter."

Their eyes stayed locked as he leaned down and kissed her, not as passionate as he had before, but it affected him just the same. When he broke the kiss, he rested his forehead against hers.

"Thank you," he said softly.

"Anytime," she smiled. "When do we need to leave?"

He pulled back and kissed the tip of her nose.

"Ma said to be there at seven. It's about a twenty-minute

walk." He glanced at the clock on the mantle. "I'm sorry I was so long. I needed to help with a couple of births."

"Hey, vet tech, remember?" She giggled. "You don't have to apologize. I understand."

"Thank you," he said. "I'm going to jump into the shower."

"Take your time. I'm perfectly content. I found a good book."

"Oh? What are you reading?"

"Keera O'Shea's latest. And I am beyond jealous you have a signed copy."

"Oh? Do you have the book?" he asked as he headed for the bathroom.

"No, it's yours. I just finished *Rum Casket.* Didn't get a chance to purchase *Davey Jones' Locket* before everything happened."

"Yeah, she went back to St. Lucia with her husband to celebrate their twentieth wedding anniversary a couple years ago. They honeymooned there. Since then, she's been on this Caribbean murder mystery bent."

"How do you know all this?"

"Well... because she is my aunt."

He tossed over his shoulder as he walked down the hall.

"Wait, what?" She called back, jumped up, and followed him down the hall. "You can't just drop that bit of news on me and walk away!"

Lachlan chuckled but turned to face her in the doorway, one hand holding the door and his other arm resting above his head on the casing.

"What do you mean she's your aunt?"

"Technically we're second cousins but she was basically raised as a sister to my da' and his brothers and sister. So naturally we all call her *Auntie* Keera."

"And that's how you have advanced copies?"

"That's how I have *signed* advanced copies. And not to mention her husband's uncle who raised him is T.S. Jameson."

"No way," she replied. "Now I know you're teasing."

"Am not," he answered. "Check out the bookshelf again. Look for *Royally Cooked* in the Js for Jameson. Flip it over and check out the picture and bio on the back." Winking, he moved away from her and slowly shut the door as she stood there, mouth agape, and the most adorable expression of envy and shock on her face.

Lachlan walked with Corinne down the steep path to High Street and toward his parent's cottage. Oscar walked beside them, slow and steady. When Lachlan had checked his wound earlier, he was happy with the progress and thought a bit of fresh air and exercise might help him heal all the more.

The wind was strong, and the sky overcast, but the storm had dissipated. The main break the town was worried about, had been reinforced with sandbags and some men were removing them as they passed by. The hair on the back of Lachlan's neck stood on end and knots clenched his belly. Looking around to see what caused his body to react so violently, he locked eyes with one of the men removing the sandbags. Though he was older, a bit rougher and filled out more in the chest, Lachlan would never forget that face. It was a face that haunted his nightmares.

The man looked down and away as another, older man walked up to him. The older man and Lachlan locked gazes and the other's eyes widened in recognition. Lachlan hadn't realized he stopped moving, until he nearly jumped out of his skin at the gentle touch on his arm.

"Lachlan?" It was Karin's voice. She was there. He whipped around to see her standing beside him. She was there. He could have cried tears of joy. "Lachlan, are you all right?"

Karin's image faded and Corinne stood before him. He looked all over for his wife. When he couldn't find her, he was drawn back to the man at the breaker wall. Karin wasn't there because of him.

"Who is that?" Corinne asked.

The man looked over again, a look Lachlan couldn't decipher on his face.

"Lachlan?"

"Nobody. He's nobody. Let's go." He gripped her elbow and hurried on through Main Street feeling the man's gaze bore through his back.

Chapter Eighteen

Lachlan's steps were hurried, and Corinne faltered a couple times in his haste. Oscar padded beside them unfazed, but Corinne could see something drastically changed when he saw the man at the breaker. They knew each other and not for a good reason.

Clearly not wanting to talk, Lachlan only slowed when they reached a cottage. The stone house stood with numerous others near a gothic looking church. His grip on her elbow increased as she saw his eyes dart toward the cemetery. Part of her worried about him, but the other part wanted to help him through whatever it was. The door of the cottage opened, and an older woman stood with a wide smile and open arms.

Her face fell when she saw Lachlan. "Honey? What's wrong?" She asked

"Nothing," he stated and pushed his way through. Corinne waited at the stoop, but Lachlan continued into the house not stopping to introduce her.

When he was out of sight, the older woman turned back to her.

"You must be Corinne," she smiled.

"Yes, Mrs. O'Quinn. Thank you for the invitation to dinner."

"It's Rachael, love," she corrected. "Come in. Come in. Do you know what happened with Lachlan?"

"I'm not altogether certain," she admitted allowing Lachlan's mother to loop her arm in hers. "We were walking together; he was happy and then..." she glanced up to see several other people in the living room watching them. Lachlan was nowhere to be seen.

"Hold up, everyone, introductions later," Rachael steered her down the hall and as soon as they were alone, she locked eyes with her. "All right, what happened?"

"We were walking over; he was a little nervous seeing the cemetery but nothing like this. Then, we walked past the breaker wall. There was a man there helping and... It all happened so quickly. Lachlan froze and stared at him. The man looked away from him, but it was clear they knew each other. After that, Lachlan wasn't the same."

Racheal nodded slowly. "Let me ask... Did the man have blonde hair?"

"Yes."

"About five foot ten?" she asked. Corinne nodded. "And

was there an older man with him?"

"Yes, so you know him too?"

"That was Beau. He killed Karin. He caused the accident that killed her and Hope, their unborn daughter. He just got out of prison. The older man is his father. He's a fisherman and they volunteered to help with the sandbags. I hoped my son would never have to see him again."

"Oh my God," she breathed. "No wonder he's upset. What can I do?"

Rachael's gaze unnerved her. It was a few moments until she spoke.

"He's probably out back," Rachael said.

Though there was no solution in her words, Corinne felt the pull to go to him. She nodded and walked past her. Finding her way to the back door, she didn't know any of the people in the living room, but they didn't try to stop her. Some even pointed toward the door.

She found Lachlan out by a small creek that ran in front of the woods. He was sitting on the bank, but he wasn't alone. A man who was clearly his father, looked over when she started toward them. Slowly walking back to the house, he smiled tightly.

"You must be Corinne," the man said.

She nodded. "Is he—"

"Best to leave him to his thoughts. Come back inside, I'll introduce you."

"Cabhan," Rachael stopped him. "Let her go to him."

"But, love—"

"No, trust me."

Cabhan nodded once and forced a smile in Corinne's direction. He stepped up into the house, but Corinne didn't pay attention to what they said. All she heard was the trickle of the water and some birds overhead. She slowly walked toward him, his back to her. Suddenly, she stopped.

"What am I doing?" She questioned. "I'm not his wife. I hardly know him."

But the moments they shared, the way he cared about her and her dog, the times they both shared their concerns, stories, and worries came back to her. The easy way he was to talk to, the fact he had not told anyone else about Karin. He was a good man. She cared for him and wanted to help him.

Go on. She heard someone say.

With a deep breath, she prayed for the right words. But her mother's advice came to her; *sometimes the right words are no words at all.* Walking to his side, she said nothing as she sat down. Lachlan didn't say anything either. His knees were drawn up, his arms resting on them and one hand clasped the wrist of his other arm. He sat still and said nothing. Corinne respected his need for silence.

Finally, his soft voice broke. "I never expected to see him again."

"Beau?" She questioned.

Lachlan heaved a sigh as if hearing the name was physically painful.

"He caused the accident."

"Tell me what happened."

"He was answering a text. He took his eyes off the road for a second but the traffic ahead of him had stopped and he didn't see it. They say he was going too fast to begin with and when he," he took a shaky breath. "Crashed into Karin's car, she didn't stand a chance. The impact broke her back in two places and the... ehm... the placenta detached. When the medics arrived, it was already too late, but she was awake and begged them... Begged them to save our baby." Lachlan's voice broke as his tears raced down his cheeks. "She begged them. I was working at the local hospital learning the human side of medicine when she was brought in. I don't honestly remember everything; it was such a blur. She begged me to save our child. She begged me to – but I couldn't. It was too late. She died in my arms on the operating table. There was internal bleeding. She died with our daughter's name on her lips."

"What was her name?" Corinne felt the tightness in her throat.

He shook his head. "I haven't said it in years."

"Please? It would do you good to say it now."

Lachlan looked over at her, his toffee eyes red-rimmed and wet. The look that crossed his face was one of pure anguish.

"Hope," he finally said. "Her name was Hope." That's all he needed. A torrent of pain flashed over his features then he cried out. Corinne grabbed him to her and held him as he wept. "My little baby. My child. I never got to see her open her eyes. I will never walk her down the aisle at her wedding. I'll never go to a father-daughter dance. I'll never know her laugh, her cry, or her voice. I'll never hold her again. I'll never... Never... All because he answered a damn text." He couldn't go on. His voice broke and he wept.

Corinne held him as he cried into her chest. Her own tears mirrored on her face.

"Lachlan," she said softly. He finally looked up at her. "You may not have those experiences with Hope, but you love her, and she was wanted and loved, even for her short life. Some people never get the love of a father. You would have given her the world, but she was your world. Remember her. But don't let it cut you off from everything else. She was an innocent child, honor her and your wife. Think of the sacrifices Karin made. She had to live through feeling her child die inside her. She was helpless to save that precious life. She died and part of you died too, but you can't honestly tell me Karin would want you to make yourself sick and keep living this half-life. No, she would want you to live for her and Hope. Hope's name is enough for you to know to live every day with their love filling you. I know. Believe me. When I lost my mom… I was so angry. It was so easy to blame my father, his drinking, his gambling, but it was so much more difficult to forgive him and live for her.

"She gave me a reason to live, a reason to be thankful every day for the life that flows within me. Yes, I did the hardest thing I ever had to do. I forgave my father. I forgave him for myself, but also for his sake and my mother's. Beau has to live every day with the knowledge, he caused the deaths of not only a woman but a child. He gets up every day wondering why it wasn't him. Why he walked away. He served time, of course he did, but he will be serving the rest of his life in a prison of his own consciousness. Don't give yourself the same sentence. It will only make *you* suffer, not him."

Lachlan stared at her for a long moment. He cupped her face with both hands and kissed her. "Whatever storm brought you into my life, I will always be thankful for it."

Her smile widened and kissed him lightly. "Me too," she said. "Come with me. Come with me to the cemetery. Say hello to them both."

Lachlan took a deep breath, but locking eyes with her, he nodded.

Chapter Nineteen

Lachlan heard Karin's voice in Corinne's truth and as difficult as it was, after dinner, he and Corinne went to Karin's grave. Armed with a bouquet of his mother's roses, Corinne at his side, he took the first step toward the cemetery.

Five steps away from the gate, he stopped. His legs refused to move; his heart raged. It would be the first time he would see her name on the headstone. He didn't remember picking one out and for a brief, horrible moment, he wondered if there was a marking at all. Then, he remembered his father telling him they put two roses on the stone every Sunday and he breathed easier.

Corinne slipped her hand into his and gave it a squeeze. He

looked over at her and smiled slightly. She blew into his life like a hurricane and even though it had only been a few hours, she meant so much to him.

For ten years he kept his heart encased in ice, refusing to let any emotion sway him. Egan was right. He was like that famous Vulcan; only logic drove him. But over the past few hours, a day at most, he had let something else take hold and his chest felt lighter, his heart, the traitorous organ, pumped again.

Still looking into Corinne's fathomless blue eyes, he took a deep breath and winced at the pain of exercising the muscles around his lungs. They stretched but the pain almost felt good. Then, Corinne smiled, and it gave him the strength to open the cemetery gate.

They walked together a little further and even though Lachlan expected to feel ill, there was nothing but peace. Corinne stopped and he looked down at her.

"You go on," she encouraged. "I'm right here. Take your time."

He nodded thanking her and walked on. His eyes locked on the dark marble headstone.

Karin O'Quinn and Hope O'Quinn

Beloved Wife and Daughter

Taken too Soon

For a long moment, Lachlan just stared at the two names. It felt like a dream, a horrible nightmare. But finally, he accepted what was written in stone. His wife and daughter were no more. Tears gathered in his eyes as he remembered Karin, her laugh, her smile, everything about her. How he loved to make her giggle and how compatible they were in everything. Some people made fun of them because they did everything together, but the truth was, he didn't want to be with anyone else. She was everything to him. He remembered their fertility issues and how many times they were disappointed. Until finally, one day, the answer was a yes. *Oh, what a day that was*. The years of injections and tests were all worth it, only to be ripped away.

Again, Lachlan took a deep breath. He had cried so much earlier; his body felt the sluggishness and exhaustion, but tears still gathered. He looked down at the ground, hoping to have a reprieve.

He saw the two dying roses his parents placed every week but the dying bouquet before the stone confused him. His father said nothing about laying flowers other than the two roses. He looked up and around, no one was there. Not that he was surprised the bouquet looked to be about a week or so old. The wildflowers tied in brown hemp twine was beautifully crude.

Setting his roses down, he crouched and kissed his fingers. Placing them on the stone, he rubbed the names.

"Heya, beautiful," he started. "I'm sorry I haven't been by. I didn't have the strength. You always were stronger than me. I miss you so much. I was afraid seeing your name here would make it worse. I had my hate and my logic to cover the emotions I didn't want to feel. But now, seeing it, I realize I should have come see you sooner. I know I haven't done much in these last few years to make you proud of me, Karin, but I swear to you, I will do everything in my power to be the man you wanted me to be. I'll come by more often, I promise. It's almost as if you are here and I can talk to you. God, I miss talking to you. You always knew what to say."

He turned his gaze down to his daughter's name. "Heya princess, daddy's here. I love you. I wish I had gotten to see you open your beautiful eyes, love. I'm so sorry I couldn't save you." Tears fill his eyes and he looked down to the roses to take a deep breath. Finally, he glanced back at Corinne and then to his wife's name. "Beautiful, I need to know you're okay with me... moving on. I'm not saying I will," he hurried. "But I've never been more tempted to." He sighed and thrust his fingers through his hair. "Just give me a sign you're all right with this."

A man cleared his throat softly behind him. Lachlan whirled around and his stomach plummeted when he locked eyes with him. Immediately, the man looked down, but Lachlan's eyes followed his to see a small bouquet of wildflowers tied with hemp twine.

"You," Lachlan spat. "What are you doing here? Killing her wasn't enough for you? You have to gloat and leave that?" he gestured to the bundle of flowers in his hand. "Lording it over everyone that *you* walked away?"

"I—" he started, then looked away. "I'm not trying to lord it or gloat. I—"

"Leave, before I call the Garda."

"Lachlan," Corinne was at his side. He shook off her hold on her arm.

"You what then? Leave flowers for what reason?"

"I'm sorry..."

"Sorry?" he demanded. "They are dead because of you! And you think a few flowers will change that?"

"No, I don't, but I just, I wanted—"

"What, you bastard? What?"

"I was told you moved to Dublin and couldn't... I thought maybe I could."

"Could what? Put flowers at the grave of the two people

you killed? You thought I would allow that? That I would *want* that?"

"No, I just… I wanted to say I was sorry, and I thought they deserved to have fresh flowers every day."

Lachlan saw red. He roared, reared back, and punched him; not nearly satisfied with the crunch he heard. Not giving Beau a chance to get his feet back under him, Lachlan charged him and tackled him. They both fell to the muddy ground. Beau didn't fight. He took the beating. Somewhere behind him, Lachlan heard Corinne screaming but it didn't matter. He was going to pay. Beau was going to pay for what he did.

"They should have locked you up for life!" *Punch*. "You don't deserve to be free." *Punch*.

"Lachlan, stop!" Corinne screamed.

"You killed my wife!" *Punch*. "You killed my daughter." *Punch*. "And you think a few flowers will change that?" *Punch*. *Punch*.

Lachlan had the upper hand. Beau lay sprawled out on the ground, Lachlan straddling him. Beau's face was a bloody mess.

Then big arms encircled him from behind. He flailed as he was lifted off Beau.

"Let go of me!" He shouted.

"Enough," Oisín's voice spoke harshly in his ear. He was no match for his younger brother. The arms around him didn't loosen as he saw Corinne rush to Beau, who was groaning. Corinne crouched down to check on him.

"Get away from him!" Lachlan bellowed. "Before he kills you too!"

"You're raving like a mad man, Lach," Oisín said. "Stop.

Enough's enough."

"He needs a hospital," Corinne said.

"Leave him," Lachlan replied.

Corinne shot him a look and he nearly wilted under her blaze of fury. She stood and stalked over to him. Her open palm slapped across his cheek with a loud crack.

"He wasn't fighting back. He didn't do or say anything to warrant that." She pointed back to where Beau still lay. "He was bringing flowers to a grave. He was saying how sorry he was. He was only trying to help, and you attacked him. His life is ruined already. Do you think he would put flowers on a grave if he wasn't truly remorseful? Shame on you. I know you're hurting, but dammit, it's not worth being angry all the time. Let it go! And as for leaving him? You took an oath, doctor. *Promote the welfare of all.* You already broke part of it. I will *not* see you break more. You will not make a mockery of the institution for which you studied so hard and represent to the people of County Kerry. Shame on you. Now, go home and let us handle this."

Like a bucket of ice water was dumped on his head, Lachlan sagged against his brother and stared in horror at what he had done.

"Dear god, I'm sorry," he felt his brother's arms loosen. "What can I do?"

"Nothing," Corinne was still angry at him. "Go home. Now."

Lachlan's eyes went from her to Beau and back again. Oisín released him when he nodded. With one last look at the situation, his eyes connected with his wife's name but instead of her face, when he closed his eyes, he saw only the disappointment, anger, and rage in Corinne's eyes. With what felt like his tail tucked firmly between his legs, he ran home.

Chapter Twenty

Corinne had never been angrier in her life as she was with Lachlan O'Quinn at that moment. Even the anger she felt toward her dad was dim compared to it. Her dad, she expected. Lachlan had a chance to do good in honor of his wife, but he chose to do evil and now Beau, a man who didn't so much as raise an arm to defend himself was moaning and bloody.

When the fight started, she screamed at him to stop but when it was clear he wasn't going to, she yelled for help. Two young men were walking down the street and one rushed to her aid. He was a great beast of a man. Broadly built, over six and a half feet tall, his jeans encased legs that looked like tree trunks and his arms were four times the size of her own. His dark brown hair was short, but his brown eyes were intelligent. He didn't speak as he ran to her. She pointed and he raced to Lachlan, muttering a curse before pinning his arms behind his back. The beast lifted him off Beau and held him in his viselike grip.

But as Lachlan ran back home and she hurried to Beau, the man was right behind her.

"What can I do?" he asked.

"We need to get him to the hospital."

"There's no way," he said. "The road is still blocked, and the coast guard is busy with injuries after the storm. There's no EAS."

"EAS?" She questioned.

"Emergency Aeromedical Service. Ehm… a medevac in the UK," he explained.

"Oh, right, is there a doctor in the village?" she asked. The phrase *other than Lachlan* remained unsaid.

"Doc Needlers is overly busy with everything. But… my da'. Bring him to me da'. He'll know what to do."

"He's a doctor?"

"Retired, former vet." At Corinne's nod, realizing he was Lachlan's brother, the beast lifted Beau gently and Corinne hurried after them.

Soon they were back at Lachlan's parent's house. Lachlan's mother answered the door.

"What? Jaysus, Mary, and Joseph," she gasped seeing the beast carrying a bloody Beau.

"We need, da', is he here?" Beast said.

"Aye. Cabhan!" Rachael yelled moving away and allowing them to enter. "Get him to the guest room, Oisín."

Beast, or Oisín as Corinne had found out, did as his mother said. Corinne followed down the hallway seeing Cabhan, Lachlan's father, rush toward them.

"What the devil?" he questioned. "Rae, heat some water and bring me some whiskey."

"What can I do?" Corinne asked.

"You have some training?" Cabhan replied.

"I'm a veterinarian technician," she answered.

"Aye, good. My bag is by the door, bring it to me?"

She hurried to grab it as Oisín lay Beau down on the guest room bed. Racing back in with the bag and the whiskey Racheal had handed her as she boiled a pot of hot water, Corinne went to Cabhan's side as he examined Beau's face.

"What the devil happened to you, lad?" Cabhan muttered.

"It was Lachlan, da'," Oisín stated. "Tiernan and I were walking back from moving the Americans in and I heard her yell. Lachlan was punching him."

Corinne wanted to defend Lachlan as it sounded bad the way his brother was painting it, but words died on her lips when she saw the bloody face. Lachlan had stepped over the line big time. She swallowed hard.

"Are you hurt?" It took her a second to realize Cabhan was speaking to her.

She shook her head, her throat too closed to answer.

"Good, where is Lachlan now?"

"Home," Oisín answered. Corinne looked up and forced a smile, thanking him.

"Please," Beau moaned. "I'm sorry."

"Shh, lad," Cabhan soothed. "When we're finished here, we need to speak with him. This is unacceptable."

"No, it's my fault," Beau spoke again.

"Shh," Corinne soothed. She looked over at Cabhan as he assessed Beau's torso to make sure there were no internal wounds they could not see.

"Give him some whisky," Cabhan ordered. "Not too much but enough to ease the pain. I need to set his nose and stitch up his eyebrow." Corinne poured. "Beau, listen to me, drink this and try to sleep."

"No, no," he swatted aimlessly. "Let me feel the pain. I deserve it."

"Enough now, lad," Cabhan nodded to Corinne who gave him some whiskey.

Once Beau was resting, Corinne helped Cabhan with the stitches and making the splint to hold the broken nose bone. When they were done, Cabhan told both she and Oisín to go to the living room where Racheal had laid out some tea and coffee. He would stay with Beau.

Softly creeping out of the room to not disturb the patient, Corinne and Oisín walked down the hallway.

"I'm sorry no introductions were made, Oisín, but I'm grateful you came to our aid," she said.

"No worries, I always come to the aid of beautiful women," he grinned. "And allow me to initiate introductions. I am Oisín O'Quinn, Lachlan's younger and handsomer brother."

"Handsomer?" she laughed.

"Aye, and though it doesn't sound like a word, it is," he winked. "And that's what I am."

She laughed at his bouncing eyebrows.

"Well, it's a pleasure to meet you, Oisín. I am Corinne, Lachlan's houseguest." Oscar, her wolfhound trotted over to her, nearly forgotten in all the commotion. "And this is Oscar. We were caught in the hurricane last night. Your brother helped us."

"Lucky sod," Oisín grumbled, winking at her.

She laughed.

"Oisín," his mother snapped. "Language."

"Sorry, ma," he replied.

"And why were you not at lunch with us today?" Racheal asked her son.

"I was moving the Americans in down the road."

"And it took you that long?" she sniffed him. "*And* they gave you a beer? And got lipstick on your collar?"

Oisín shrugged. "What can I say? They were generous and really *really* grateful." He grinned.

"Nonsense, you and Tiernan stopped off at the pub, so you did."

Oisín rolled his eyes and turned to Corinne. "Who needs private investigators when they have an Irish mother?"

Corinne stifled her laugh as Rachael tissed. "Enough, young man. And I have seen that saying posted on your social media. Now apologize to our guest for missing lunch."

Oisín turned to Corinne and made a show of bowing low.

"Forgive me, my dear lady. The call of alcohol at the public house was too strong for one so weak willed as I. I beg your pardon and forgiveness for not joining you in the partaking of cooked meats and stimulating conversation. Will you ever forgive me, sweet lady, or shall I fall upon my sword for such a slight?"

Corinne was shaking with suppressed laughter but when his mother smacked his arm with her wooden spoon, she could contain it no longer. Oisín grinned, though he rubbed the sore spot on his arm.

"You have been hanging out with your uncles too much," Rachael said. "But come now, Corinne, dear, have some tea. I'm sure you could use some after that ordeal. I'm so sorry you had to see my eldest son act like that."

"From what I saw, it's Lach who will need the comfort. She slapped him good and proper, so she did," Oisín said.

"It was just because he was nearly hysterical. The man I met yesterday who saved my dog and me would never have acted like that. I needed him to see how wrong he was and how irrational he was being."

"You care for him already," Rachael stated as she poured the tea into the cups.

Corinne felt a blush heat her cheeks and she looked down immediately.

"There's nothing to be concerned about, love." Rachael handed her the teacup. "Though Oisín seems a tough guy, he's a softie when it comes to women and he will not spread rumors."

"Shh, Ma," Oisín grumbled good naturedly. "You'll give away my superpower to get women."

"Oh hush, Oisín, it's very clear you won't be getting this woman, so you can give your opinions freely without thinking about getting in her pants."

Corinne nearly choked on the tea.

"Sorry about this," Oisín teased her. "Ma loves getting into everyone's business. My family calls her Grandma Deirdre two point oh. My grandma was the town's busybody."

"Don't talk about your Gramma Dee like that, Oisín."

"I'm not saying anything anyone else hasn't said," he sipped his tea.

"You said *was*," Corinne spoke up trying to get the conversation off her. "She's passed?"

"Aye, she and my grampa Orin passed a year ago. They were married for nearly forty-five years."

"That's wonderful," Corinne said. "Not that they passed but that they were married for so long. Was it sudden?"

"No," Rachael replied. "Orin had a heart condition after his first heart attack twenty-five years ago. He passed peacefully a year ago with all of us surrounding him. And Dee, god love her, couldn't cope without him. She passed six months later."

"I can't fathom that depth of love," Corinne said. "I don't believe my father ever really loved my mother. And when she died, dad seemed almost relieved."

"I'm so sorry for your loss, love," Rachael replied. "How long ago?"

"Five years," she stated. She looked at Oscar resting near the hearth. "Oscar was hers. She got him when he was a puppy." Her wolf hound looked up at her.

"He's such a handsome lad," Rachael said.

"What brings you to Ireland, Corinne?" Oisín asked.

Corinne looked up at him. "Well, no offense, but you clearly have an English accent. I'm just curious why you were driving during a hurricane."

"It's a long story."

"We have time," Rachael offered.

Corinne broke out in a cold sweat. She didn't want anyone else to get involved. "I would love to tell you, but I don't think Lachlan should be alone in the state he's in. I should be getting back." She set the teacup down and stood.

Not missing the look between mother and son, she gathered her handbag. Oscar lifted his head and she patted her thigh. He slowly got up and ambled over to her.

"Well, thank you for taking care of my son's outburst, Corinne," Rachael said standing. "I hope we can talk more later."

"I would like that, Mrs. O'Quinn."

"Rachael, please, love," she said.

"Rachael and forgive me for ducking out so quickly. I hope you understand."

"I do, dear," she replied with more meaning behind those little words than Corinne could decipher. "But at least take Oisín with you. He can protect you if Lachlan is still violent."

"Lachlan would never hurt me," Corinne stated.

Rachael smiled softly. "No, he wouldn't. But still. Oisín, go with her."

"No really, not necessary," Corinne walked to the door with Lachlan's mother, Oisín following behind.

"She's pimping me out again," Oisín winked.

"Oisín," Rachael snapped. "Manners."

"Please let me know how Beau is doing?" Corinne asked.

"Of course," Rachael said. "And let us know if we can help you and Lachlan."

"Thank you."

"You have a good heart, my dear," Rachael spoke gently. "I'm glad he found you."

Corinne smiled but stepped outside without another word. She looked across the street to see the three paths leading in different directions. When they walked to dinner the sun was setting, now it was dark, and Corinne wasn't sure which path to take. She stood there staring at the three ways to go, Oscar stood beside her. She heard the soft; "Oisín, go." But didn't pay attention to it until he came up beside her.

"This way," he grinned. "And what sort of gentleman would I be if I allowed a young woman to walk home alone in the dark?"

"I don't know, when you become a gentleman let me know," she teased.

Oisín barked a laugh. "Aye, that's me all right, lass, your Irish Rogue."

Corinne laughed again. "Can I ask you something?"

"Of course," he answered, as they started down the road she hadn't seen as an option along with the three paths.

"*Aye* and *lass* are very Scottish. I know the Irish do use them occasionally, but there are also times your accent changes slightly. Why is that?"

"I'm impressed you can hear the difference," Oisín said.

"My father is from Glasgow. The Scottish accent is very familiar to me."

"Ah, I see. That explains somethings. I studied in Scotland for university. Aberdeen."

"What field of study?"

"I double majored in Applied Mathematics and Civil and Structural Engineering."

"Impressive," she replied. "What did you want to do with that?"

"Initially I wanted to be a builder," he explained. "But after I saw the pay scale, I realized that wouldn't work for me and decided to create my own company."

"What do you do?"

"I own and manage a moving company."

"Of course, that makes sense. You said you were moving the Americans in."

"So, you were listening," he teased. "I sometimes wonder why we men always get the reputation of not listening to things when women seem to have the same affliction most of the time."

"Probably because we listen the first time and it takes you men fifteen times hearing the same thing to realize we're talking."

"Harsh and cynical," he replied. "I can see why my brother likes you." Oisín laughed but Corinne's heart did a flip hearing the fact that Lachlan liked her from someone other than Lachlan himself.

"Truthful, I think is what you meant," she said, proud her voice didn't waver though her adrenaline was spiking and she felt like she could run the whole way to Lachlan's arms and stay there forever. It was far too soon but she had never felt the sort of pull she felt with him. He was quickly becoming an addiction. Though it had only been a day or so, she missed him when he wasn't nearby and could not wait to see him again.

Oisín spoke beside her and they carried on a pleasant conversation, but her heart and mind were only partially in it. And when Lachlan's cottage came into view, her breathing sped up and she walked faster toward the door.

Chapter Twenty-One

Lachlan heard the front door of his cottage open and looked up. He sat in the armchair by the fireplace, his knee bouncing uncontrollably. Corinne and Oisín walked in. He stood and rushed over to them.

"How is he?" Lachlan asked concerned. His eyes moved between Corinne and his brother.

"Well," Oisín began. "His face is a pulverized mess."

"Oh God," Lachlan groaned. The horror of what he had done had poured over him like molten lava as soon as Corinne slapped him and as he waited in the cottage for her return, he went over the events feeling worse every second.

"I should go to him. See if I can help." He made a move for the door, but his brother stepped between them.

"I don't think you're particularly wanted right now. Besides, da' has everything well in hand."

"You took him to da'? Good." Lachlan breathed a little easier. "I can't... I don't know what came over me. Seeing him there, knowing he was the cause of it all, I—"

"He wasn't the cause of it all," it was the first thing Corinne had said. He looked over at her. "It was an accident, Lachlan. He's done his time. He has to live every day with the guilt and horror of what he did. He was only trying to make amends and you beat him up. He didn't fight back, and you didn't stop. What kind of man do you want to be? The kind who acts rashly and regrets? Or the kind who is logical and thinks before he reacts? Tell me. Was he causing any harm? Was he vandalizing their grave? Was he hurting anyone being there? With flowers he handpicked for your wife and daughter? No, he wasn't but you were. You caused this. The man I know, the man who methodically took care of my dog when he was injured, the man who spoke to me so kindly when I was scared, the man I've grown to care for, wouldn't behave like that. I don't even know you and I know that's not like you."

Lachlan and Oisín stared at her. Eventually, Lachlan licked his dry lips and looked away. "You're right," he turned from them and looked into the fire. "I've placed the blame on him for so many years. I've hated him, cursed him, hurt him, and it wasn't his fault. He was a dumb kid and yes, it took Karin and Hope away from me, but it ruined his life. I blamed him because it was easier than to say it was an accident. It was too hard to think something so pointless took them from me. Now, I see my grief is no longer grief, it's poison and it's poisoned too many people, myself especially. I don't want to live like this anymore, Corinne."

There was silence behind him until Corinne walked around to face him.

"Then it's time to let it go," she took his hand in hers and held his gaze. "Let it go, Lachlan. For all our sakes but yours especially. Let it all go. Never let *them* go, but let go of your anger, hate, hurt. Let it go, Lachlan, let it go."

She pulled him close and pressed her lips to his. He knew in that moment nothing else mattered. He had closed himself off for far too long, he had forgotten what he was missing, and it took Corinne and her dog being blown into his life to make him live again. He knew it wasn't the best kiss he had ever given, as desperation took control and he felt their teeth click against each other's in their haste. But it was by far the sweetest. They didn't hear Oisín letting himself out until they finally pulled away and looked toward Oscar who had wiggled his way between them.

Lachlan gazed into her eyes and saw something reflected deep inside, an image of the man she deserved, a man he would do his damnedest to become. Her eyes glazed with a look any man knew. She was asking him to make her his. The look grew and he swallowed hard. Not only was she innocent, it had been a very long time for him. She deserved better.

She did not give him a chance to answer, instead she took his hand in hers and slowly, her eyes never dropping his gaze, walked backward to his room. As soon as they stepped over the threshold, she dropped his hand and sat on the bed.

Lachlan stood in the doorway, his heart pounding in his chest as he watched her. She did not look nervous, in fact of the two of them, he was sure he looked more like the shy inexperienced virgin. Corinne licked her lips, took a deep breath, and in one swift move, pulled her shirt over her head. Lachlan's mouth went dry.

"Are you..." He finally cleared his throat. "Are you certain?"

She nodded. "I want to be with you, Lachlan. I've never met anyone like you and no one I've ever wanted more."

"But," he was desperate. "Your first time should be cherished and given to someone you care for."

"I'm looking at the only man I've cared for in this way. And I know just by your words, you will cherish me. I don't ask for more, just this. Please. There's something between us. I can't name it I don't know what it is, but I want it to grow. Make love to me, Lachlan. I want you." Sweeter words had never been spoken.

He stared at her for a long moment. His mind warred with his heart. Finally, seeing vulnerability enter her eyes, he threw off the doubt, fear, and concern. He wanted her to. He would be lying if he denied it. Though they had only just met, he felt a connection with Corinne that rivaled any other. The thought of someone hurting her, abusing her, taking what she was freely giving him, boiled his blood. He would cherish her, protect her, keep her safe from harm, and love her if she allowed him to love her the way he knew he could. She was his future as she helped him work through his past. She was the song of his heart's desire.

With that thought, the side of his lips ticked up and he stepped inside the room. Her eyes lit with excitement and a touch of nerves. The look endeared her even more and as he walked slowly to the bed and sat beside her, he tucked a piece of hair behind her ear.

"You give me a gift, Corinne," he began. "I will treasure it and I do not take it lightly. It is yours to give and I am honored you chose me. If at any time you want to stop, all you have to do is tell me. No judgment, no question."

She nodded her understanding and ducked her head as a blush colored her cheeks. "I may seem confident, but I'm shaking."

"We do not have to do this."

"No, I want to," she answered. "I just don't know what I'm doing. I mean, I *know* obviously, but I don't know."

Lachlan found himself grinning. "Do you want to wait? Just a little bit? Let me make us some dinner? You can relax."

She blushed red and looked away from him. "I could do with a few minutes," she said. "Can I take a quick shower? Maybe use your razor?"

Lachlan chuckled and gently slipped his hand under her chin, pulling her face to look at him.

"You are beautiful just the way you are. I don't care about any of that, all right? But if it would make you feel better, yes, you absolutely can use my razor. Why don't you stay here for a second, let me draw you a bubble bath and make something for dinner?"

"A bubble bath does sound heavenly," she said. Lachlan leaned forward and kissed the tip of her nose. "But this isn't cancelled, simply postponed," she stated.

"Not cancelled," he agreed. "I promise."

With a nod and a quick kiss, she let him stand and go into the bathroom. Lachlan shook his head at the stupid grin he saw on his face when he caught his reflection in the mirror. Turning on the water to the tub, he went through the recipe for his favorite dish. He had all the ingredients and excitement coursed through him at the thought of sharing it with her. His one regret was he didn't have a bottle of wine to go along with it.

As he filled the steaming water with the bubble bath he found from god only knows where, the familiar smell made him smile. It wrapped him in comfort, and he felt a soft kiss on his cheek. His heart filled with joy when he realized it was Karin's kiss. It was her familiar smell. It was her way of telling him it was all right; the sign he had asked for so desperately at the grave.

"Thank you, beautiful," he said softly. "I'll never forget you but it's time."

He saw a flash of her smile in his mind's eye. More pressure lifted and he took a deep breath, the pain nonexistent. As he turned back to the sink, his ring caught the light of the few candles in the room. He froze as he stared at the golden metal. There was no way he would be able to do what he and Corinne wanted to do while Karin's claim wrapped his finger.

With a deep breath, he took hold of the ring and slowly worked it off his finger. "I love you. I will always love you," he whispered as the ring popped off around his knuckle and a weight lifted off his shoulders. His stomach roiled for a moment as he stared at it. He had never taken the ring off since Karin had placed it on his finger on their wedding day. But, pocketing it, he huffed. "It's time," he repeated and grabbed his razor. As he set it on the side of the table, he caught his face in the mirror. He was smiling. Without another thought, he called to Corinne. "Bath is ready, love."

He heard movement and looked toward the door. His jaw promptly dropped when he saw her. She had pulled off her jeans and stood in a pink bra and underwear set. He swallowed audibly when a salacious grin spread across her face.

"Reminder, O'Quinn. Postponed, not cancelled," she said.

"P...P... Post... Postponed... aye, absolutely," Lachlan stuttered.

Her grin widened and she walked up to him, picking an invisible piece of lint off his dark brown sweater.

"Make me something good to eat, O'Quinn," she whispered huskily. "I'm famished and need to keep my strength up."

With a wink, she slipped between him and the tub and reached around to unhook her bra. Coyly looking over her shoulder, she caught his gaze.

"Are you going to watch me?"

He shook himself out of his stupor and hurried to the door. "I'll be in the kitchen, if you need me."

"I told you how I need you already," she replied.

Lachlan nearly tripped over his feet as he walked out. Stopping, he took a deep breath, calmed his nerves, turned with a grin, and winked.

"Later."

Her smile widened as he backed down the hallway. Once out of her eyeline, he shook his head but couldn't stop the smile. His hands shook with excitement and some nerves as he pulled out his phone. He knew he wanted to make his steak and kidney pie, but he needed one special ingredient he didn't have in his pantry.

Lachlan: You busy?

Oisín: At the pub, what's up?

Lachlan: I need your help. Can you get a couple bottles of that wine I brought over for Christmas last year?

Lachlan: Oh, and a box of condoms?

Oisín: Wine and condoms? Are you finally breaking that celibacy streak?? Yeah! Get you some, bro!

Lachlan: I'm serious, Oisín. Please.

Oisín: Okay, okay, when do you need it?

Lachlan: Now.

Oisín: Damn, can't I finish my beer?

Lachlan: Please, Osh. I don't have anyone else I trust to do this.

Oisín: Well, damn, flattery will get you everywhere.

Oisín: The wine I remember but remind me the size condoms you need. Small? Medium?

Lachlan: Kiss my arse.

Oisín: Small it is. Be there in 10.

After rolling his eyes at his brother's inane jest, Lachlan text back.

Lachlan: You're joking, I hope.

Oisín: Always!

Lachlan: Good. Don't knock. Text me when you get here.

Oisín: Now entering stealth mode.

Lachlan chuckled. His kid brother was always messing around. But he was grateful for his friendship and help. Lachlan's mind and body hummed. He went to the kitchen and pulled out the ingredients for the dinner.

Chapter Twenty-Two

Corinne couldn't stop her grin. She had never been surer of anything in her life and she also had never been more nervous. Taking her phone, she needed to talk to the one man who knew her better than anyone.

The phone rang six times before Geoff's voicemail picked up.

"Geoff, give me a call back? I really need to talk to you. You know how we talked about that *card* I needed to give up? Well, it's happening. I really need you to call me back. Love you, babe. Call me."

She hung up and slipped further into the warm bath water. When Geoff hadn't called her back in five minutes, she blew out a frustrated breath and grabbed Lachlan's razor.

Soon, delicious smells filled the room and Corinne's fingers began to resemble a prune. Draining the tub, she rinsed off and dried quickly. Looking at herself in the mirror, she grinned and put on some fresh makeup. Her hair dried quickly even without a dryer and she pulled on a little black dress Geoff was determined to get for her birthday the year before. Her black pumps completed the outfit and she walked out of the bathroom to see Lachlan pouring two glasses of red wine. He looked up and a slow appreciative smile lifted his mouth.

Oddly, she expected nerves to set in but when they didn't and she only reacted to the heat she found in his eyes, her toes curled inside the pumps and a blush crept up her neck.

"You look amazing," his low voice caressed her, and goosebumps broke out on her arms.

"Thanks," she finally said. "You too."

His jeans fit far too well, and the button up mossy green shirt made the toffee color of his eyes pop. The look on his face captivated her. It was exactly the look she always dreamed someone would give her when she decided to finally be with him. Lachlan's reaction to her cemented her decision and when he walked toward her, almost hesitant, she knew she chose correctly.

"We don't have to do this. I want to, don't get me wrong," he said quickly. "But I want you to know, you have all the power here. If you want to back out, we will stop. No questions asked."

She stared at him for a long moment, then took a step

toward him. Her hands shook and she felt her stomach twist into knots. But she took his hands that rested at his sides, looked up into his eyes, and everything fell into place.

"I have never been surer of anything in my life, Lachlan."

Without another word, she slipped her hands up his arms and to his shoulders. Intertwining her fingers behind his head, she leaned up and slowly brushed her lips over his. Lachlan did not react; he merely closed his eyes. When she pulled back, he looked at her, his pupils dilated so much the toffee color was nearly gone.

"Lachlan," she started. "Can dinner be kept warm?"

He nodded.

"Good," she whispered against his lips. "Then, Lachlan O'Quinn, take me to bed. Please."

Lachlan said nothing for a long moment. He closed his eyes briefly, took a deep breath, and when he opened them, Corinne grinned. Determination and affection tinted the orbs.

He said nothing, only took her hand gently in his and kissed her knuckles. As his gaze locked with hers, he nodded. With a gentle nudge, he walked them toward the bedroom, shutting the door behind him.

Chapter Twenty-Three

Lachlan held Corinne close to his side, staring up at the ceiling. His fingers gently stroked her exposed back, as hers toyed with the dusting of hair on his chest. Dinner long forgotten after nearly three hours in bed, Lachlan had gotten up and brought the wine in when it was clear neither wanted to get up.

The was wine nearly finished and the moon shone through the drapes. They listened to the rhythmic crash of the waves on the shore. The first time together, he could sense her nerves though she tried everything in her power to prevent them from showing. He took his time, even though he felt as if his entire body would combust, but it was worth watching her.

She moved in his arms as if she was born to be in them. A wholly contented smile lifted his lips as he squeezed her hip. She looked up at him, her eyes making his insides do a flip.

"That was…" she began. He waited. He'd like to hear words like *incredible, amazing,* or *indescribable* but he wouldn't push it. He knew he was rusty. So long as she was — "Magical," she said.

Magical? He questioned and his male ego puffed out his chest. *Damn straight.*

"I'm glad," he answered tamping down his reaction.

"I hope… it was… good for you?" she blushed bright pink in the moonlight and he had to chuckle as he moved her face up to his.

"Better than good, love," he answered.

Her face lit as she beamed.

"But now, are you hungry? Tired?" he knew what he was but deliberately refused to say the word. She needed rest. She looked up at him again, a sheepish look clouding her eyes.

"I am a little of both," she admitted.

Lachlan smiled and tapped her hip. "Stay here, I'll warm up dinner."

She shook her head. "I want to watch you."

He chuckled as he pulled the sheets off him and stood. He offered his hand. "Come then, love. I'll do my best to make a show for you."

Winking, he closed his hand around hers. She beamed and leaned back to grab her phone from the nightstand.

"Whoa, hey now," Lachlan teased lowering his hands to cover the important bits. "No pictures."

Corinne exaggerated a pout. "Even one? Just for me?"

Lachlan laughed and shook his head. "Reality is so much better."

"True," she debated. "Fine then. No pictures... for now."

Shaking his head, he grabbed his underwear and quickly pulled them on.

"No fair!" she complained.

"You'll be rewarded if there's no pictures," he teased.

She pulled her lower lip between her teeth to prevent a grin. It did little good and Lachlan caught himself thinking how beautiful she was.

"No pictures, promise," she said.

"Good, join me?"

She nodded and pulled off the sheets. She grabbed his t-shirt and pulled it over her head. His brows rose in question.

"Who knows who might come by. I wouldn't put it past Oisín to conveniently drop by," she started.

"I wouldn't either," Lachlan chuckled. "I'll bar the door."

She giggled and walked with him to the kitchen. He pulled the food out of the cooler and lit the wood in the stove. Just once, he wished he had a more modern stove that he could leave the pies inside to heat up without having to monitor them.

Corinne slipped onto one of the seats at the kitchen nook and watched him. Oscar padded over and lay at her feet. She then glanced down at her phone. Out of the corner of his eye, Lachlan saw her mobile light up and heard the faint buzz.

Looking over when she didn't answer it right away, he saw

her staring at the screen.

"Everything okay?" he asked.

She glanced up and nodded quickly, too quickly. He knew he shouldn't pry but after everything they just shared, he wanted her to know he saw her more than a quick piece of fun.

"Corrie," he started and waited until she looked up. "If it's something important…"

"Oh, no," she sighed. "Thank you, Lach, but no. It's nothing," she took a breath. "I met a man on the ferry coming over here. Gave him my number and he's texted me twice, again just now."

Lachlan hated the feeling that exploded in his chest. Jealousy.

"He's someone I thought I'd try out the new me on and now, I just don't want him texting me, but I don't know what to say. I'm not good at this sort of thing and he's a nice guy. But…"

"But?" he had to dampen the bite in his tone.

She locked eyes with him. "He's not you."

The tight ball in his chest loosened when he heard and saw her sincerity.

"Block his number," he offered.

"Yeah," she replied. "I guess that's the easiest, but he hasn't done anything to warrant me ghosting on him."

"I'll text him if you want," he offered. "I know how guys think."

"Would you?" she asked.

"Of course," he answered. "Here, give me the phone." She

did and he saw the short string of text from the guy named George.

Typing out a quick, simple but nice rejection text, he sent it before she had a chance to see it. The consolation he had was, he didn't see any of her replies. The guy may have texted her three times, but none of those had a response. He may only have known Corinne for a couple days but within those days, she had wormed her way under his skin and into his heart.

Never in his life before had he ever believed in love at first sight or, as his grampa used to call it; *lightning.* But looking into Corinne's eyes, he could honestly say, he understood. He understood it all and that scared the shite out of him.

Handing her phone back, he stroked her cheek and went back into the kitchen.

"I wonder why Geoff hasn't messaged me," she said finally.

"Was he supposed to?" Lachlan asked.

"Well, I called him when I was in the bath... I wanted to talk to him."

Lachlan glanced back and laughed when he saw the look in her eyes. "About me?"

"About... what we were planning on doing. But he didn't answer, and he has not texted me, which is not like him. When I need him, he answers or calls me back right away."

"I'm sure he's fine, love," Lachlan answered pulling the pies out of the oven. "He'll call."

She nodded as he placed one pie in front of her and pulled out some sparkling wine Oisín had picked up along with the red. Corinne practically bounced in her seat when she saw it. Oscar had lifted his head looking for scraps and as Lachlan poured the champagne into two plastic flutes Oisín had remembered to get since Lachlan had no wine glasses, he watched her give Oscar a few nibbles of the steak and kidney pie. Sitting opposite her, Lachlan couldn't believe his good fortune.

They ate together laughing and talking about everything and anything that came to mind. Soon the champagne was finished between them, dinner mostly done, and the clock on the mantle read after midnight. The conversation lulled at just the right moment and Lachlan rested his hand out on the table, palm up. Corinne eagerly slid her hand into his, froze for a moment, and looked up at him.

"You took your ring off?" she questioned.

"Yes," he answered. "I needed to. There was no way I could..."

"What is it, Lach?" she asked. His eyes were still on their clasped hands.

He looked up at her and sighed. "I was just thinking," he admitted.

"What about?"

"About us," he revealed and smiled. Her face lit. "Corrie, I... I don't want to scare you away, but I also want to make sure I don't miss my opportunity to tell you... I would like to continue this. I don't know what your plans are, if you will want to go back to England or if you would..."

"Would what?" she prompted when he didn't continue.

"If you would want to stay... here... with me," he finally said.

"Stay?" she questioned. "I hadn't thought long term about any of it," she admitted. He stroked her knuckles with his thumb. "But I do know I would love to stay with you. There is only one thing holding me back."

"Anthony Rossi?" he asked.

She nodded. "He'll never stop looking for me. I couldn't put you or anyone in danger."

"You can't run for the rest of your life," he stated. "We could go to the English police. I'm sure Scotland Yard has the Rossis under surveillance. We can talk to them together."

She thought about it for a moment but when she locked eyes with him, he saw her answer.

"Okay," she whispered, and realization washed over him. His lips spread into a grin and the corners of his eyes crinkled.

"Okay?" he questioned.

"Yes, okay,

if you'll have me. I'd love to stay with you."

He let out a whoop of excitement and stood quickly pulling her into his arms. "I promise it'll be okay. We'll go to London together, check on Geoff and go to the police. I promise."

She nodded and though her smile was a mile wide, he still felt her hesitation. Rossi had been cheated of his prize; her. He would not take kindly to that.

All would have to be well, he thought as his mouth captured hers in a scorching kiss.

Chapter Twenty-Four

Lachlan woke a few hours later to his phone ringing. Corinne was tucked warmly against his side, her head resting on his chest. She moaned and flipped over when he moved to grab the mobile and answered without checking the ID.

"Hello," he cleared his throat. "Hello?" he said with more authority.

"Lach?" he recognized his cousin Trevor's voice. "That you, man? You sound different."

"Hey, Trev, yeah it's me," he leaned up on his elbow. "What's up?"

"You sure you're all right? Sounds like you just woke up. It's well after ten there, isn't it?"

Lachlan looked at his phone's time and blinked. He never slept in. The fact he was on-call twenty-four-seven, didn't help but he usually was at the clinic before seven.

"Yeah, I'm good, mate," he answered and, with a glance at Corinne still asleep, he stood and left the room. "After the storm, I wasn't really needed. Took the morning off," he never lied to his cousins and hated it, but it was all he could say.

"Oh, sorry, man, didn't mean to wake you."

"Nah, no worries, what's up?"

"Well, Peter called me yesterday," Trevor spoke of his cousin Peter Carlisle. "He told me Geoff called him, you remember Geoff Ainsley?" Trevor questioned then went on before Lachlan could say anything. "He was asking about you. He said it seemed a little off but thought I could see if everything was all right. He said something about a girl?"

Shite, he would have to tell him. "Ehm… yeah, mate I'm sorry I lied to you… just now."

"Lach, what's going on?" Trevor was serious.

Lachlan huffed. "There is a girl. A woman, of course," he corrected. "Her name is Corinne."

"What?" Trevor gasped.

"I know it's strange but—"

"No, no, her name?"

"Corinne," Lachlan repeated.

"Oh," Trevor breathed. "Sorry, man, it took me off guard. I thought you said… Karin."

"No," Lachlan answered, proud he didn't let his voice crack. "*Corinne*, she's—"

He was cut off when he heard Trevor's wife's voice in the background.

"Trev, I'm heading to rehearsal – oh, sorry, babe, didn't know you were on the phone," Cassie said.

"No worries, love, it's Lach."

"Oh, hey Lachlan!" Cassie called.

"Hey, Cass."

"I'll leave you boys to your talk. I'll be home a little later today. We're getting drinks afterwards."

"Have fun. Be safe, love. Call me?"

"I will," Lachlan heard a soft kiss through the speaker. "See you tonight."

"Break a leg," Trevor called after her. After a beat, Trevor spoke again. "Right, sorry, man. Cass got a part in a new musical. Rehearsals started first of the month."

"I'm happy for her. She sounds happy," he said as he made some coffee on his French Press.

"She is, it's a brand new show interpretation of the *Mayor of Casterbridge*, so competition was heavy but anyway, back to you. You said her name's Corinne."

"Yeah, she's from London. Her best friend Geoff is Peter's friend from the military. He wanted to double check since we only met once. She's... had her fair share of bad guys."

"There's more, I can hear it in your tone."

Cursing the fact Trevor knew him so well from the years

they spent meeting up for dinner or a pint in Dublin where Trevor went to school, Lachlan sighed.

"There's more, aye, but I don't feel right talking about it."

Trevor took a deep breath. "Peter said she's in some pretty deep shit. I just wanna make sure you're—"

"I'm fine, Trev. Thank you, but I'm good."

"All right, so long as you swear."

"I swear," Lachlan chuckled.

"Whoa, what the hell?" Trevor's shocked voice stopped him. "What the hell was *that?*"

"What?"

"You honest-to-god laughed!"

"Yeah, I guess I did."

Trevor paused for a moment, then said, "Corinne?"

"She's... helped."

"Wow..." his voice trailed off. "Man, are you... falling for her?"

Lachlan took a long moment before he answered. "Yeah, I am."

Trevor whooped in excitement and Lachlan winced. Pouring the now finished coffee, he took a deep inhale. Too hot to drink, he needed a caffeine infusion if he was to handle his cousin's excitement.

They spoke for another ten minutes, Trevor asking questions about Corinne, but some Lachlan dodged. He wasn't going to tell his cousin everything.

Once he hung up, grateful Trevor had a call from his agent come in, Lachlan turned to the bedroom door. Corinne stood there, grinning, arms crossed over her chest, his white t-shirt falling just to her mid-thigh. Her hair, slightly mussed, fell to her shoulders and her eyes were bright.

"Who was that?" she asked.

"My cousin Trevor."

Her eyes grew wide. "The singer? I would love to meet him again. What is it with you guys? You have some pretty famous family members."

Lachlan shrugged. "Lucky, I guess."

"You said your aunt was Keera O'Shea, the author?"

"Yes, well, technically second cousin. She and my Uncle Paddy, her husband married when I was about fourteen. Her mother is my grandfather's sister. Auntie Keera basically grew up with our family. I call her aunt and her husband uncle even though they aren't technically that. Their kids call my parents and the others, aunts and uncles."

"How many family members do you have?" she asked, accepting the coffee mug from him, and wrapping her fingers around it as if warming. They sat before the fire after he stoked it to life and added more peat. She tucked her feet under her and leaned into him.

Lachlan wrapped his arm around her and counted quickly. "Uncle Emmet and Aunt Mara, Uncle Innis and Aunt Trish, Uncle Sean and Aunt Ness, Aunt Keera and Uncle Paddy, two aunts and uncles on my ma's side. Then those not by blood but as a respect of who they are; Aunt Char and Uncle Derek, they're Peter's parents and Trevor's mother's sister but they have come over here a lot so we all just started calling them aunt and uncle."

"Wow."

"And then my two dozen or so cousins and my two sets of grandparents before Grampa Orin and Grandma Dee passed. It's a crazy holiday season."

"I bet," she replied resting her head on his shoulder. "I was sorry to hear about your grandparents. Your mum and Oisín told me."

"Thank you. We were close."

"I don't have any extended family. My parents were either an only child or estranged."

"You've got us now," he rubbed her arm and kissed her cheek. When she didn't answer right away, Lachlan looked down at her. "What's wrong?"

"This has all moved so fast. I guess I'm waiting on the hammer to drop. I can't make any commitments until I know you and the others would be safe."

"I am and so are you."

"I'm not so sure. I'm getting worried about Geoff. He hasn't called me back and when I tried him again, it went straight to voicemail."

"Listen, love," he changed the subject. "I need to make my rounds and check in at the clinic. Want to join me? It would beat sitting here with nothing to do."

Oscar ambled toward them and waited for a scratch behind his ear. "Yeah, I'd like that. I also want to check on Beau and make sure he's all right."

Lachlan's throat suddenly went dry. "I should probably check in with the Garda. He has every right to press charges."

"He does, but he said he wouldn't," she kissed his jaw. "You're safe."

"Thank god for small mercies, I guess."

"Agreed. I'll go get dressed." She made a move to stand, but Lachlan held her to him. "We should get going." She grinned.

"In a bit," he began. "I didn't get a chance to show *good morning*."

"Show? Don't you mean say?" she leaned back into him. He shook his head, took her empty mug of coffee, and promptly began to show her *good morning*.

Chapter Twenty-Five

Seeing Lachlan make his rounds in his *doctor mode* was endearing. He had one face and tone for the people, which was *no nonsense* and another for the animals which was calm and empathetic.

The occasional times he looked over at her and winked made her heart flutter. She never felt more cherished, loved, or complete than when she and Lachlan made love. He was gentle yet commanding and she loved the way he made her feel.

Geoff's silence still bothered her and the text from George, though sweet and nice, didn't sit well with her. She knew most men didn't get subtle, but she hadn't texted him back at all. Pulling out her phone, she scrolled through the texts.

George: Hello, beautiful. I hope you made it to the hotel. I was hoping maybe we could meet up and have dinner. If you're interested. I enjoyed talking to you.

George: Hey, I'm in Mayo County. Wasn't sure if I was anywhere near you but I'd love to take you out!

The third text was a picture of him on the Cliffs of Moher. Then she read the text Lachlan had sent.

Corinne: Hi George, while I'm flattered by your attention, I'm no longer interested. Thank you for understanding.

She had to admit, the text was perfect, and George hadn't texted her since. She glanced up to see Lachlan finish with his client and walk her way. His smile lifted the cloudy thoughts swirling in her mind. She stood from the chair and greeted him.

"How did it go?" she asked.

"Slight foot scald, nothing major but it was the fourth ewe to come down with it. Farmer O'Neil was concerned."

"Antibiotic spray and a foot bath?" she offered.

His grin grew. "Aye, exactly."

"Did you tell him to change out the straw bedding often to prevent it from becoming wet and warm? That's a main contributor."

Lachlan fought the smile lifting his lips and Corinne looked down, away from the temptation.

"Aye, I happened to mention it," he answered and took her in his arms forcing her to look up at him. Not that she minded. "Sexy and smart. How did I get so lucky?"

She wrapped her arms around his neck.

"By being the sweetest, dearest, moronic, stubborn, intelligent, kindest, imbecilic, man I've ever known."

"Getting mixed signals there, love," he teased.

"Then let me make it clear," she took his face between her hands and kissed him in front of the farmer, ewes, and God.

When they pulled back, he nodded slowly. "Starting to get a clearer picture."

She giggled and kissed him once more, quickly that time. When she stepped back, she watched as Lachlan waved to the farmer and picked up his medical bag. Taking her hand in his, they walked down the path to the main gate. Once through, Lachlan squeezed her hand.

"I'm glad you came with me."

"Me too. I miss working with my vet. She was so knowledgeable and kind to everyone. I'm glad Geoff told her I didn't just run off. I hope she forgives me."

"I'm sure she will, love," he wrapped his arm around her shoulders. "Any word from Geoff?"

"None," she answered. "I'm worried."

He said nothing and she wasn't sure if his silence meant he no longer believed everything was all right or he was tired of saying it.

"How about lunch?" he asked.

"How many more clients do you need to visit?"

"We've finished the most pressing and I need to check in at the clinic after lunch. Not that I'll have many clients."

"Okay, *that* tone has a story behind it," she said. "What's wrong?"

Lachlan huffed a sigh. "There's this woman, Old Widow McKeel. She spread a rumor about me that's damaging and of course, a lie." Corinne let him think a moment not speaking. He sighed. "Apparently, according to my da', she's tried it before, but I haven't handled it, yet. I guess I somewhat wanted it to either go away on its own or let it become so bad I had to leave and go back to Dublin. But now, I realize I don't want either to happen. I'm... happy here and with you."

"I'm happy too. What rumor? What did she say?"

"The crazy woman called me out to check on her horse, who was fine, but when I looked back at her, she had pulled her top off. I got out of there pretty quickly and she claimed when she offered to pay me for my vet services, I told her I would take payment in sex."

"What?" Corinne gasped, then giggled uncontrollably. "Seriously? And people bought it? Do they know you at all?"

"No, they don't. All I know is, visits to the clinic have dwindled and the day of the hurricane I had no patients. And the few we visited, and I went to see yesterday, weren't as welcoming."

"Did you talk to your dad about it?"

Lachlan nodded. "He said I need to get her to confess, but I don't know how, nor do I want the issue."

"But you need to," she stated. "I agree with your dad. If she's done this before, she needs to know she can't do this again. You have every right to be here and see your practice thrive. The rumors and lies of one individual should never change that."

Lachlan raised her hand to his lips and kissed it. "God, how I love your tenacity. Don't let us run into her today," he chuckled. "You just might be the one to put her in her place."

"I would. And she wouldn't know what hit her. I may not look like much but I'm strong."

They stopped walking and turned toward each other.

Lachlan's heated gaze caressed her skin. "You look like everything I've ever wanted. And trust me," his voice was a low rumble that elicited goosebumps on her arms. "I know exactly how strong you are." One of his eyes closed on a slow wink and Corinne couldn't wait any longer. She pressed her body to his and captured his lips with hers. Their kiss quickly turned heated and though her stomach growled wanting food, all she could think of was the man before her. She wanted him more than any other. But when Lachlan broke the kiss, both panting for air, he rested his forehead to hers, again his toffee colored eyes were dilated.

"Let's go to lunch," he said rubbing her nose with his. "Before I take you home and feast on you."

Her cheeks heated but she grinned. "Sounds perfect."

Kissing her nose, he took her hand in his and they walked toward the village.

Lachlan led Corinne to the pub off the main street. When they entered, a roar of a few patrons drew their attention. Six men, his brother included were huddled at the bar, watching the hurling game on the television. The roar, it would appear, was because there was a technical foul on the Kerry team.

Lachlan chuckled, shook his head, and found a small two seat table by the front window. Stepping up the one step to the raised platform, he pulled out her chair and sat opposite her.

"Is that Oisín?" she asked.

"Aye, and his group of miscreants," Lachlan said. "Did he tell you he owned a moving company?"

"He did, on the way home after your parent's dinner."

"Those are his friends from Uni and employees. I tell him not to mix the two. I mean, what happens when he has to let one of them go? They hang out as friends too much and it becomes awkward."

"I understand both sides," Corinne began. "On one hand yes, you are absolutely correct. It would be awkward but on the other hand, there's no greater loyalty than friends and family. Wouldn't that bond make them want to make it the best? Be the best?"

Lachlan debated, then nodded. "You're right. I never thought of it that way," he reached for her hand. "You're amazing, you know that?"

She grinned.

"You're right, Lachy," Oisín's drunken voice came from beside him as his arm draped over Lachlan's shoulders hanging on him. "She is a keeper... mmm... have you two, *you know*," he exaggerated a whisper and then whistled a quick low wolf whistle.

Corinne immediately looked down and blushed profusely. Lachlan wanted to punch his brother or at least pinch his ear and pull him away like their mother used to but refrained.

"Oisín," Lachlan started. His brother's drunken gaze fell on him. After seeing the glassy look in his eyes, he sighed. "How many have you had?"

"Ooh," Oisín's eyes grew wide as his hand came to cover his mouth. "Shite, daddy, I promise I've only had like a..." he lifted one hand and quickly counted, once he ran out of fingers, he waved away. "A couple. Don't punish me... but she can," he winked.

Lachlan rolled his eyes. Oisín started giggling and slapped a hand on Lachlan's shoulder a little too hard. "Just making sure you put those condoms to good use. If not, I'd be happy to for you. Though we might need to go up a couple sizes."

"Oisín, stop," Lachlan ordered seeing Corinne's cheeks darken even more.

"Stop what?" Oisín looked genuinely confused.

"Talking."

Oisín laughed even more, almost falling over as he did. Lachlan's quick movement saved him from hitting his head.

"All right, that's it. You've had enough," Lachlan took his brother's arm and put it around his shoulders.

"Ooh, hey, handsome," Oisín teased then gripped his brother's chin and turned toward Corinne. "Seriously, who could refuse this face?"

"Come on," Lachlan said then caught Corinne's eyes. "Will you be all right while I get him home? I'll be right back."

She nodded. "I'll be fine."

Lachlan thanked her and began turning the great drunken beast that was his kid brother. Lachlan swore under his breath. "Did you do steroids or something? No one, other than Uncle Emmet is built like you. And even he isn't as big." Though Oisín was proportionate to his six-foot five-inch frame, he had the type of body most men only thought about and most women swooned over.

Oisín giggled but spun around, nearly taking Lachlan down with him and leaned over to Corinne.

"Hey, I just want to say, thanks. You made my big bro smile for the first time in a decade and also, I really like you, even if you are English. Be sure not to break his heart."

"Come on," Lachlan said trying to turn Oisín back and lead him down the stairs. He felt Corinne's eyes on him as he left and hoped Oisín hadn't hurt her or scared her off.

Chapter Twenty-Six

Oisín's words rang in Corinne's ears as she watched Lachlan maneuver his brother out the door and into the street. Their parent's house, where Oisín still lived wasn't far but as they faded from her view, she heard a woman near the bar, scoff. Her blood ran cold when she looked over and saw an older woman shake her head.

"Just like those O'Quinns. Can't hold their liquor and when they're drunk, god help *any* woman near them."

"Come now, Fionnula," the bartender called. "You know that's not true. The O'Quinns have been pillars of our town since me da' was wee."

"All I'm saying is, when Lachlan O'Quinn cornered me in Donovan's stall, I could smell the stink of whiskey on his breath."

"That's a lie," Corinne stood and barked. "Lachlan is a professional and a gentleman. He would never drink while working and he sure as hell wouldn't want you like that. He has some standards."

"How dare you?" Old Widow McKeel stated. "What on earth is this English whore doing here anyway?"

"I may be English by birthplace, but my mother was Irish from Connemara and my father is Glaswegian. So, the only *whore* here is you," Corinne replied. "How many good men have you ruined or attempted to ruin? You can't get anyone willingly into your bed, so you lie about being assaulted? That's what makes women who have a legitimate assault claim, not be believed because hags like you *cry wolf* and there's no reason behind it. From what I heard; Lachlan nearly threw up when you whipped off your top to proposition him."

"Shut your mouth, little chit," the older woman demanded.

"Not until you admit to lying about a good man."

She scoffed again. "She's clearly in love with him and therefore is blind to his nefarious ways. Anyone here think I'm lying?" She looked around the room and no one spoke up.

Corinne stared at the patrons and the pubkeeper. "None of you will stand up for him? How dare you. His family has been in this community for generations. His father took care of all your animals. He lost his wife and child here and yet still came back when you needed it. When you needed him, he answered the call. You should all be ashamed of yourselves. Lachlan O'Quinn could be anywhere with anyone, but he chose to come back here, even though he had nothing here to hold him and all he had was bad memories and you add to it? You treat him like an outsider, lower than dirt. You act as if this woman runs this town. When all I see is a sad, bitter, old hag who likes to stir up gossip and lies. You take her word over one who has done no harm, only good. You take the word of someone who has *cried wolf* about this before? You should all be ashamed of yourselves. Lachlan O'Quinn is a great man. You don't deserve him."

When no one spoke, Corinne looked over at Old Widow McKeel, a smug smile lifting her lips. "Don't involve yourself in things you don't understand, child. You will always lose to age and experience." She turned away from Corinne, effectively dismissing her.

"You're right," Corinne continued softer. "Those are two things you have more than me: *age* and experience. Experience in tearing down good men. I feel sorry for you." She slowly turned back to look at Corinne. "Sorry, because you will never know the absolute freedom and bliss found in Lachlan's arms. And yes, I may be biased because I *am* falling in love with him, but I pity you. You must be so lonely and in need of attention that you make up those stories about people. Well, you go ahead and find your next victim because I will be with Lachlan. I will be sharing his bed, and I will be the one he comes home to when people like you try to tear him down. You know where I'll be... where will you?"

The entire pub was silent, apart from the television still playing the game. The woman shook herself out of her shock and looked around the room. Everyone was staring at her. She finished her hard cider and cleared her throat. Setting the glass down on the counter, she walked stiffly to the door. Only then did Corinne see Lachlan had returned and was standing in the doorway. Fionnula McKeel stopped and looked up at him, his face expressionless.

"Let me pass," she demanded.

Lachlan didn't move for a moment, but he eventually

stepped aside. She walked out the door, head high and her back ramrod straight.

The pub was still quiet until one of the patrons called to Lachlan from the back. "My work horse threw a shoe the other day, hasn't been walking right since. Think you could take a look, lad?"

Lachlan paused a moment, then glanced at Corinne, the corner of his mouth ticked up. Looking back at the farmer, he nodded.

"I'll swing by later today and have a look," he said.

"Will you be keeping office hours today, doc? My setter hasn't been himself lately and threw up last night," another patron said.

Lachlan nodded. "Aye, after lunch, I'll be in the clinic. Bring him by."

"You're a good man, yourself, Lach," another person said. Lachlan nodded in thanks and slowly the pub's liveliness returned. Lachlan walked up to Corinne. Before she said anything or sat back down, he pulled her into his arms and kiss her. The patrons cheered, raising their glasses in the air toward them but Corinne didn't hear much more as her mind, body, and soul were consumed in a kiss and the truth of what she felt for Lachlan O'Quinn crushed down on her.

She loved him.

Hearing Corinne stand up for him against Old Widow McKeel, gave Lachlan a sense of pride he hadn't felt in a long time. But hearing her confirm to the old crone that she was falling in love with him, stopped him in his tracks. He didn't have long to revel in the mutual feeling stirring in his gut. Fionnula McKeel knew she'd been beaten and to see it was exhilarating. Corinne was magnificent and to see and hear her speak so passionately cemented his feelings and her place in his heart.

Instantly, he wanted her in his arms. He wanted to carry her back to his cottage and show her how he felt. But as soon as McKeel left, Farmer Shaughnessy called out to him. He had to force himself to pay attention to what he was saying instead of watching how the light danced across Corinne's freckles. It warmed him more than he cared to admit hearing the patrons of the pub ask for his services. Seldom shaken by any gossip or scandal, the thought of ruining his father's practice and good name was worse than any defamation to his character. But it was over... thanks to her.

Corinne had made it all happen and as he held her in his arms, lips on hers, he knew he had found home. Finally letting her go, he smiled and waved to those who were cheering. Soon, they sat back together at the table and the pubkeeper walked over with a Guinness in one hand and a glass of white wine in the other.

"Ah, Colin cheers, mate," Lachlan said. "Can we put in for a couple sandwiches?"

"Aye, the drinks are on the house," Colin answered. "I'll get those started for you."

"Thank you," Corinne replied taking the white wine and smiling at the pubkeeper. Lachlan took his pint after Colin left and held it out to her to toast.

"Thank you," he said.

"For what?" She asked.

"For... everything," he admitted. "I was dead inside until you blew into my life. I was rough and brusque with everyone until you showed me that showing kindness wasn't going to kill me or make me regret. Showing me everyone I care for isn't going to be taken from me. For standing up to me. Slapping me when I was an idiot. Standing up *for* me to strangers and people who would rather see me torn down than shown kindness. For being you. I... love you, Corinne."

Shock registered first on her face but soon concern replaced the surprise but only for a split second, then joy, pure, radiant, and complete lit her face.

"Really?"

"Really. I know it's only been... god, a very short time. But my grandfather, dad, and uncles all talked about this thing called lightning when they found their wives, I felt that with you."

"I felt that with you, too." She sighed a happy sigh and raised her glass to his. "I only just realized what I'm feeling for you isn't just lust... though there's plenty of that," she wiggled her eyebrows and he laughed.

"I've created a monster."

Corinne shook her head. "She's always been there, you just made it all right for her to show herself. But it's not just that. When I heard that woman speaking about you like that, my blood boiled. I wanted to, no, *had* to defend you. And it was because I'm in love with you. All of you. Everything about you."

Those words washed over him like a healing balm, patching up the pain and loss, never fully forgotten but dulled and made precious.

"You have no idea how those words make me feel," he said.

"Yeah I do," she answered.

He reached for her hand and intertwined their fingers. She was his future and he loved looking at her.

Chapter Twenty-Seven

Corinne was floating. She understood what everyone meant when they said being with the man they loved, even just watching as he worked, was precious. She knew she would never get tired of watching him or being near him. He was like a raft in the sea and she wanted his comfort, needed to be near him. He had her assist him in surgery and clinic duties. She never thought when she boarded that ferry and waved goodbye to Geoff, her life would be better than ever. Her only concern was why hadn't Geoff called her back. It had been three days and not a peep.

As Lachlan finished with his sixth patient, he removed his surgical gloves and threw them away. Taking a deep breath, he turned to her.

"I haven't been this busy in the clinic since my first week," he smiled softly and stroked her cheek with the back of his fingers. "And it's all thanks to you, love."

"You have the talent, Lach," she answered. "I'm just here to help."

"You do more and *did* more, you know it. You singlehandedly beat Old Widow McKeel at her own game and you have been invaluable to me."

"That wasn't my intention. I just wanted to defend you."

"And you did," he kissed her lightly. "Thank you."

"You are very welcome," she smiled and wrapped her arms around his waist. "How is Oisín, by the way?"

"He'll have a splitting headache when he wakes up, so he will. But he basically passed out when I got him home. I wouldn't want to be him when Ma gets ahold of him. But I did see… Beau while I was there. He was just leaving after staying over for Da' to help with his injuries. He looked terrible, but da' assured me he was well. I feel horrible. I told him how sorry I was and how I would understand if he pressed charges against me. But he told me he understood why I did it and was sorry. He said he would not pursue legal action. We… I guess came to a truce. He offered to stop laying flowers on their graves, but I refused, telling him it was a nice thing to do and I wouldn't mind it."

"Oh good," she breathed. "I'm so proud of you."

His arms tightened around her, pulling her closer to him. She took in his scent, some of the light ocean cologne he sprayed before he left still clung to his sweater, and something entirely Lachlan blended to make a very enticing scent.

After a beat, Lachlan spoke low, his voice rumbling in his chest, against her ear. "There's something worrying you, love. I felt it all afternoon. Is it Geoff?"

She nodded and pulled away slightly to look up at him. "I don't understand what happened. He's never done this before."

"I know, I'm sorry."

"Aren't you going to tell me everything will be all right?"

He looked down at her. "Is that what you really want to hear?" Corinne thought a moment, then shook her head. "I didn't think so." He kissed her forehead.

She leaned her head up to his, an invitation. Just as his lips brushed hers, someone knocked and opened the door.

"Oh! Forgive me, doctor," his secretary was closing the door quickly.

"No, no, Donna, come in," Lachlan pulled away from Corinne and though she understood, she missed his heat.

"I didn't mean to interrupt," Donna said opening the door a little wider.

"You weren't," he soothed.

"Your next patient is ready," she answered. "Mr. Burke's setter."

"Thank you," Lachlan extended his hand for the file on the ill dog. When Donna handed it to him, he smiled. "Thank you, Donna. I appreciate it… you. I appreciate all you do."

Her eyes widened and Corinne watched as the corner of her lip ticked up.

"You're welcome, sir. And may I be so bold as to say, I am incredibly happy for you and Ms. McDonnagh. If there's anything I can do to help, please let me know."

"Thank you," they both said.

"And send in," he looked at the name on the file. "Padme."

"I will. Would you like a cup of tea, Doctor?" she offered.

Lachlan froze and Corinne's brows furrowed.

"Thank you, yes, I would love one," he answered. "I take it just like my father likes it." She smiled and left the room.

"Tea?" Corinne questioned.

"It's a long story," he answered. "I'll tell you tonight."

Another knock separated them and as Padme entered with her owner Mr. Burke, Corinne sat back down to watch Lachlan and to lend a hand if needed. One thing she was certain of, nothing could make her leave Lachlan's side.

Chapter Twenty-Eight

One Month later

Lachlan woke to Corinne's phone ringing on the nightstand. He reached beside him, but his hand only met cool sheets. Leaning up on his elbow, he flicked on the light. Over the past month, he had electricity installed, a radio, and a television. With Corinne at his side every day at the clinic and in his bed every night, he had more reason to spend time at home. Without basic lighting, his oil lamp and candle inventory ran low quickly.

Grabbing her phone, seeing he just missed a video call with Geoff, he threw the sheets off him and raced out of the room.

"Baby?" he called.

She jumped and turned to him with the smile he always loved. But he said nothing only offered her the phone. She shrieked when she saw the name.

"I'm sorry I didn't get to it in time," he said.

She shook her head and unlocked the phone. Trying to call Geoff back, it went to voicemail. She shouted in frustration. It had been over a month since she had heard from Geoff and all her texts went unanswered. As soon as she clicked off the second attempt, tears gathered in her eyes. She looked up at him and the look in her eyes gutted him.

"I'm sorry, baby," he soothed and took her in his arms. She melted into him and cried. Her hands gripped his arms and she shouted in frustration.

Lachlan held her close, allowing her to cry. As soon as her sobs slowed and softened, she pulled back and wiped furiously at her face.

"Ugh," she grunted. "I know something is wrong. Something is terribly, terribly wrong."

"I know, love," he sighed. "I am so sorry."

She shook her head and stroked his chest to wipe off her tears. He stilled her hand and waited for her to look up at him.

"I love you. And we will get through this."

She nodded and held him closer. "I know, but I'm beyond worried."

"I know you are." For the past month they had fallen deeper in love with each other and though he knew beyond a shadow of a doubt she loved him, he always sensed she was distracted by Geoff's absence. Even calls to Peter and Vivian revealed nothing and when it was clear their relationship was on the rocks, Lachlan and Corinne stopped calling to ask about Geoff.

"Hey, why don't you take a nice hot bath? Hmm? It'll help you. I promise I'll answer it if he rings back."

She shook her head. "I already showered last night. I just need my coffee. I'll be all right." She forced a smile and patted his unshaven jaw. "Thank you." She leaned up to kiss him.

He watched as she walked back to the counter and picked up her mug of coffee. Taking a couple small sips to test the temperature, he saw how tired she was. Usually, he chalked it up to their fun in bed, but today, he saw the rings around her eyes and knew there was more. She was worried, terrified something bad had happened. Kicking himself for not seeing it before, he vowed to help her through whatever it was. She was who his heart sang for, his heart's desire, and he'd be damned if he let another woman suffer while he stood by and did nothing. Even their quick trip to London two weeks ago to speak with Scotland Yard yielded nothing. The Police Constable took their information and promised to call if something was found. But they hadn't heard anything from the police.

He huffed a silent sigh and went to pour himself coffee. Being Saturday, they had slept in until nearly eleven, but he planned on checking in on some animals he had treated over the last couple weeks.

Since Corinne's defeat of Old Widow McKeel, his clinic was overrun with checkups on animals whose owners believed the lies and refused to visit him. He had more apology gifts than he could count. Not that he blamed them, they didn't know *him,* and he didn't exactly make it easy for them to take his side. But the practice was flourishing, and he had the trust his father always spoke of. Donna even made him tea every day and he counted that as a win.

His eyes drifted back to Corinne who sat down in the armchair by the fireplace. Oscar moved to sit in front of her. If only Corinne could have the same peace he felt. Maybe there was something he could do. Maybe they could go to London and look for Geoff again.

It was an hour later when her phone rang. She screeched. Oscar jumped up and barked. Lachlan ran out of the bathroom where he was shaving, dressed for his house calls.

"It's him!" Corinne cried and answered. "Geoff?" But even if Lachlan hadn't seen the screen, he would know from her wail what was happening.

Chapter Twenty-Nine

Corinne stared in horror at the screen of her phone. Geoff's number video called her, and she was beyond glad he did, but when she accepted the call, the scene that greeted her turned her stomach.

Geoff hung, chained by both wrists, making his body look like a Y. His head hung low; his knees bent. He was stripped to his tight black briefs and his feet were resting in a dog pan filled with water. Blood, both fresh and dried covered his chest, arms, and legs. Two men stood, dressed in black on either side of him.

"Geoff?" she squeaked. He moaned and his head moved slightly. *Thank god*, he was still alive. "Geoff?" She said a little more forcefully.

The screen flipped around, and she saw black specks in the corners of her eyes as she recognized the man holding the phone.

"Good morning, Corinne." The voice and evil look on the face didn't match who she remembered. "What's wrong, my dear? Don't you remember me? Oh, how sad. I did enjoy your text. But I would imagine it wasn't you who sent it, am I right?" he looked past her. "Come into view."

She felt Lachlan come up behind her and place a hand on her shoulder.

"Better," he stated. "Handsome. What's your name?"

Lachlan didn't answer.

"What..." she began. "What do you want? Why... why have you hurt Geoff?"

"I want you."

Her brows furrowed. "Why? We only met on the ferry, George. Why would you want me?"

"Oh, no, my dear," he chuckled. "You mistake me. I don't want you for *me.* No no no, I'm merely the collector. My client wants you."

Her gut clenched. "Anthony Rossi?"

"Got it in one," he grinned. "You gave me the slip somewhere on the N52. I was surprised. You must have lost a tail before. I knew cloning your device would help me. But after the towers were down due to the hurricane. I couldn't find you. Once you called Geoff here, I had your position on the coast, but you hung up before I could see where exactly. Hence the texts. When I realized you weren't falling for it, I had my lads here pick up your beloved Geoff. He's been my guest ever since."

"Hate to see what you'd do to your enemies," Geoff's voice was soft, but she heard it. George chuckled and flipped the screen around so she could see him. Geoff's face was bloodied and bruised but he still looked toward the screen. Corinne covered her mouth as a whimper escaped.

"What do you want?" Lachlan demanded.

"Not too bright, is he?" George spoke but they couldn't see him as the screen was flipped to Geoff. "It'll be an exchange. You, for Geoff's life. He's a strong one, none of the torture we've used this past month has worked. He still won't tell me where you are. I am thinking fingernails or toenails next. Have a preference?" Geoff's nostrils flared as his chest expanded in a deep breath, but he showed no fear. "I figured before I do and mess up his pretty mani-pedi that no straight guy should have, I would call you."

"It's pretty relaxing, you might try it sometime, scrape off that toe fungus you're sporting," Geoff spoke, his voice stronger than before. George chuckled.

"So, what do you say, Corinne? Five years of your life for the rest of your friend's?"

"Don't do it, Corrie," Geoff commanded.

George tsked and motioned one of the guards. One of the men dressed in black took a step forward and punched Geoff.

Corinne cried out when Geoff's head snapped to the side but was so proud when he looked back at the guard and spat in his eye. The guard tried to punch him again, but George's voice stopped him.

"I do hate to be interrupted. Now, where were we?" George contemplated for a moment. "Oh, yes. What do you say?"

Corinne stared at the screen seeing Geoff stare straight ahead and into the camera. He shook his head slightly. Lachlan's grip on her shoulder increased and the black speckles in the corners of her eyes grew.

"Maybe this will help," George said and looked back at one of his guards. The man turned and there was a whirling sound. The guard held a device in his hand. Corinne couldn't make it out but as soon as he was close enough, he placed the device on Geoff's chest.

There was a crackling sound and Geoff shook uncontrollably but made no sound at first. Finally, he let out a scream of pain as smoke rose from his body. Corinne shrieked and tears fell down her cheeks as she watched her best friend be electrocuted. Everything else faded away.

"Stop!" She roared.

George held up a hand and flipped the screen around when the buzzing stopped. "Made up your mind?" he asked.

"I—" she stopped, realizing she was panting and couldn't get enough air in her lungs. "I—"

George raised an eyebrow, waiting. "He can't take much more, Corinne. He's already at thirty milliamps. For every second you delay, another is added."

"I—"

"Thirty-one."

"I—"

"Thirty-two."

"Stop!"

"Thirty-three."

"Okay!"

George cocked his head to the side. "Okay?"

"Yes, okay, I... I accept. Just let him go!"

"No," Lachlan said beside her. She didn't look up at him.

"I'll let him go, once I deliver you to Mr. Rossi," George said. "Where are you?"

"No," she shook her head. "I'll come to you. Where are you?"

He paused then agreed. "Meet me back in London. I'm sure your father is eager to have you home."

His sick grin had her heart racing. "What did you do to him?" she demanded.

"Dear me, I didn't think you cared since you left him to rot."

"He's my father."

"He is," George conceded. "He's alive. That's all you get. Now, shall we say two days? At Battersea Power Station."

"Fine," but it wasn't fine. And as certain as she was her choice would wash over her later, at that moment she was strong. "But you have to promise me, no more torture."

George debated. "No more," he agreed. "But know this, if you try anything, go to the police, try to run again, I will have them attach the device to your bestie's testis and leave it on at thirty-three, your lucky number and leave him to rot. Believe me, he will suffer before his heart will eventually explode. Do I make myself clear?"

Corinne nodded as Lachlan's grip on her shoulder increased. "Let me talk to him. Please, it may be the last chance I get."

Sighing, George stared at her for a long moment, then eventually looked over at Geoff.

"Say anything about where you are, and I'll tie Corinne up to the electricity beside you. Understood?"

Geoff nodded once and looked into the camera. Only then could Corinne see how gaunt he was. His cheek bones were sharp against his skin, his eyes, what she could see from the one that wasn't swollen over, were bloodshot, his nose was broken with dried blood caked on the bridge, and his lip was swollen and a dark red cut bisected the lower one.

"Geoff," she choked. "Oh my god, I'm so sorry."

"I'm okay, honey," he tried to smile. "Do me one small favor?"

"Anything."

"Tell Peter I'm sorry. I never forgot Afghanistan. I never told him I loved him, and I wish we had gotten a chance to be together instead of just being friends. We both felt the attraction, but I let him go and I shouldn't have. I loved getting to know him in that Germany hospital."

Corinne licked her lips. "You can tell him yourself when you get out."

He shook his head looking dejected. "All those sleepless nights we just talked about everything, likes, dislikes, how I always made fun of his favorite thing. How I held him when he was scared after he was a POW. I never slept so well as I did those nights with him in my arms. Tell him I'm sorry I never told him how I felt. Please, promise me. It's... it's the anniversary and I didn't call him. He has PTSD and if he doesn't hear from me today... he..."

"Okay, okay, it's all right," Corinne soothed. "I promise I'll tell him."

Geoff tried to smile. "Love ya, honey. I'll get you away from that bastard."

George turned the camera around. "Oh, I should tell you, Anthony Rossi has changed the terms. You try leaving or anyone tries saving you, your father will lose his hands."

Corinne gasped. "Monster."

"Hey, I'm just the delivery guy. Got a problem with the pizza, talk to corporate. Now, I'll be seeing you in two days."

The phone screen went blank. Corinne didn't move. She didn't feel Lachlan walk to the decanter of whiskey, pour two glasses, and walk back to her. She didn't feel him crouch in front of her until he pressed the glass into her hand and take the phone from her other one.

"I… I don't know what to say," she finally said.

"There's nothing to say," he replied. "It's not going to happen."

"Lachlan, you heard what he said. If I don't, they'll kill Geoff and hurt my dad."

"And so? Did your father think of you when he made that bet?"

"No, but I'm not him. I care about my actions. If I don't go to Anthony, Geoff will die a horrible death. I can't let that happen."

Lachlan leaned forward and cupped her face. "I love you and I will help you. I will not allow that monster to hurt you, Geoff, or your father."

"You can't promise that. You're only one man."

"One man with a large army behind him," he said. "You're

an O'Quinn now, love. You have us all behind you."

She searched his gaze. "What are you saying? I'm not an O'Quinn. They owe me nothing."

"They owe you everything. I'm here today because of you. I love you and I hope one day we can change that last name of yours. But until then, know beyond a shadow of a doubt, you are an O'Quinn."

Corinne closed her eyes refusing to hope. But then something Geoff had said rung in her ears.

"It's May..."

"Ehm, what love?"

"The month, it's May, right?"

He nodded.

"Geoff and Peter were discharged in October. Halloween. It's not the anniversary."

"He didn't say discharged, love. He said the anniversary of Peter being saved from the Al Qaeda camp. Trevor's talked about it. He was a wreck when his cousin was captured." Lachlan nudged her to drink the whiskey. She took a sip but shook her head.

"One, neither of them ever admitted feelings for the other, right?"

"Not to my knowledge, you said Geoff's had girlfriends, Peter's engaged to Vivian. They're straight as far as I know."

"Geoff is bi. But he's never said anything about... having a relationship with Peter. Why would he say all that stuff?"

"War? Army? I know some guys who aren't into men but when you're cooped up in the barracks... things happen." Lachlan finished his whiskey.

"Maybe so, but then why did he tell me that now?"

"Could it be a message?" He asked indicating the glass for her to drink again.

"Maybe, I need to call Peter."

Corinne set the whiskey down and took her phone from where Lachlan had set it on the table. Finding Peter's contact information, she dialed.

Chapter Thirty

Indianapolis, Indiana

Peter unlocked the front door of his home, seeing the Red Line Bus barrel past. He and Vivian had picked the little bungalow off College Avenue in Indianapolis because it was close to their favorite places in Broadripple, an eclectic area of town just north of downtown and near Butler University.

They both fell in love with the cute front and the layout. The backyard, however, was like a jungle and it nearly deterred Vivian, but Peter swore to build her the dream backyard; paved patio, fire pit, pergola, garden, stone path, grill and eating area. And from the sounds of voices happening outside, the men began their work early on Saturday.

"Babe?" he called out.

There was no answer. Pulling out of his running shoes, he set the coffees he had grabbed from their local shop after his run, on the kitchen island and grabbed a grape from the cluster Vivian had out. Following the sounds outside, he stopped short when he saw Vivian out on the raised cement slab that served as the original backyard space, talking to the foreman. They were laughing at something and Vivian placed a hand on the contractor's arm. The man grinned and looked up at her. Jealousy raced through him and Peter saw red.

Stalking out the open sliding glass door, he walked past Vivian who greeted him and pushed the contractor away.

"What the hell do you think you're doing?" Peter demanded.

"Uhm…" the contractor looked at Vivian.

"Don't you dare look at her," Peter ordered. "I hired you to do a job, not flirt with my fiancée. If you are incapable of that, I suggest you pack up."

"Peter," Vivian's touch instantly calmed him. "It's on me, babe. I started talking to him. Come on, let's go back inside."

Peter never dropped the contractor's gaze but eventually allowed Vivian to pull him away. Once they stepped up into the kitchen, Peter stalked to the living room as Vivian slid the door closed.

"What was that about?" Vivian questioned.

"As if you don't know," Peter fumed.

"Enlighten me."

"You gave me so much shit last month about my concern for Geoff to the point I was scared to come home, worried you changed the locks on me. We worked through it but now, I come home to see you flirting with some sweaty contractor and I'm supposed to be okay with it?"

"First off, I wasn't flirting with Tim. He said something funny and I laughed. You know I'm a touchy-feely person. It meant nothing. Secondly, Tim isn't someone I buried feelings for and then lied to my fiancé about."

"I was confused. You know what happened in the hospital after Afghanistan."

"So? Your anger is misplaced."

Vivian's nonchalance angered him even more. "Geoff is my best friend. Always has been," he stated. "He was there for me when I didn't know what to do or how to adjust to civilian life. Without him, I wouldn't be here. He was there for me when I needed him the most. He's missing and it's eating me alive. I can't talk to the one person I need because her little feelings get hurt whenever I mention him."

"Maybe that's because you lied about it for so long and then sprung it on me. How was I supposed to feel?"

"Oh, I don't know, understanding, maybe? "

"Understanding? Of a man who never liked me? Of someone I worry could steal you away? Of someone you always listen to more than me? Come on, Peter!"

"Oh please, I always knew you were jaded, I just didn't know you were childish too."

Vivian's face morphed into a mask of bitter coolness. The instant Peter said the words he wished them back.

"Viv, I—" he tried but knew it was futile. Vivian held up a hand stopping him, and he had to bite his cheek to stop. Taking a deep breath, Vivian's entire frame changed. She pulled herself up to her full height and the look on her face twisted Peter's stomach into knots. It was devoid of all emotion.

"Enough," Vivian finally, wearily said. "I've had enough, Peter. I can't keep pretending like I'm okay. I've been lying to myself and you for a while now. We've lost that spark, that love we used to have."

"Viv—"

"No, I know you've felt it too. It's okay to admit it, it's healthy. And I for one feel like I'm standing in the way of something. You and Geoff… I don't know… but I refuse to stop you from finding and pursuing your love or knowing who you are. I want you to be happy as I want to be happy. But I am not Geoff and I can't be him for you."

"I don't want you to be him for me, I want you to be you."

"Do you though?" There was no anger or harshness in Vivian's tone. It was simple and as the words hung between them, Peter knew the truth. Vivian would never be enough, and he would always hurt her, whether by figuring out who he was or just being friends with Geoff. The bitter truth flowed through him as he looked at his fiancée.

"I thought so," Vivian said. Peter's emotions broke at her soft resignation.

"I'm so sorry," he breathed. Vivian hurried to him and gathered him into her arms. Peter took in the familiar scent of her perfume, the feel of her in his arms, unsure if he would ever hold her like that again.

Vivian said nothing as Peter held her. Not one to ever allow his emotions to show, a single tear slipped down Peter's cheek. He mourned the loss of a good woman and a future he expected. Finally, when his breathing evened out, Vivian pulled back and looked at him. Her soft brown eyes loving. No trace of tears.

"It's strange being on this side of emotions. Is this how you men feel?" she tried to break the mood.

Peter breathed a laugh but instead of the tight ball of emotion in his chest from ten minutes ago, he felt lighter.

"I'm so sorry, Viv."

"Hey, enough of that, okay?" Vivian said. "You have every right to love someone, anyone. I'm just sorry it wasn't me."

"I do love you. I don't know what…"

"I know," she agreed. "But I could never stand in your way. What you feel for Geoff… I want someone to feel that way for me."

Peter nodded. "You deserve it and more."

"Though I have to say, seeing a six-foot-one-inch two-hundred-pound blonde Army Ranger barreling down to stake his claim on me was pretty hot."

Peter chuckled. "I didn't think about anything, I just wanted him away from you."

"And it worked."

They were quiet for a moment. "Oh, god, what are we going to do about this place? All of this?" he looked at the furniture they had purchased.

"I'll keep what I need and sell the rest. You need to get to London. I'll tell you how much we got for it and put it in the joint account. You can transfer your half to your personal account."

"No, you keep it," Peter disagreed. "It's the least I can do."

"Oh, no, sweetie," Vivian replied. "You're not minimizing our three years to paying me off. We split it equally or no deal."

Peter nodded and rubbed Vivian's arms. "Thank you," he said. "And honestly, I didn't mean what I said. You didn't deserve it. I'm sorry. I was angry."

"I know, thank you. And since we're being honest... I *was* flirting with Tim."

Peter laughed. "I knew it!"

"Can you blame me? He's hot."

Peter cupped her jaw and looked deep into her eyes. "Not at all. I couldn't blame you if you acted on it. I've been a shitty fiancé recently." They were quiet again. Vivian did not contradict his statement. "Do you think our parents will be all right with this?"

"It's our life," she answered. "Yes, they'll be fine. We haven't put more than the down payment on the venue, and I haven't found a dress yet."

He froze, then stroked her cheek. "I would have loved to see you in a wedding dress."

"Maybe one day you will. When I find the one who thinks of me as much as you think of Geoff. Who knows, maybe you and Geoff will be guests of honor at my wedding?"

Peter shook his head ruefully. "He's... betrothed, or will be, to someone he doesn't love."

"Right," she drawled. "Aristocrats and all that."

Peter looked down. But they said nothing more for a long moment. "God, we're actually doing this?"

"Yes, we are," Vivian answered allowing Peter to break away from her. "You need to go after Geoff. He needs you and even if you don't end in a relationship, he's your best friend."

Peter ignored the butterflies in his stomach that hadn't gone away at the thought of seeing him again and chose to focus on the burning question. "What if... he's missing? What if I can't find him?"

"You need to get to London first."

"I can't leave you with all of this to do."

"You can," she answered. "Besides, I can't very well flirt with Tim with you still here." She winked.

Peter chuckled. "No, I guess not." He looked down, her engagement ring catching his eye.

"I should give this back to you. It was your grandmother's," Vivian said, her voice catching for the first time.

Peter nodded slowly and watched as she worked the diamond ring off her finger. With a sigh, she offered it to him. Tears threatened in her eyes, but she cleared her throat and turned away as soon as the ring was in his palm. He felt like a bastard.

"I'm sorry."

"Stop. Stop saying that," she said, her back still to him. He let her be for a moment. She took a deep breath and he saw her hands wipe something off her face. She turned with a forced look of optimism. "Now—"

She couldn't say anymore as his phone rang. Pulling it out of his jogging shorts pocket, he recognized Corinne's number. They had been in communication during the past month looking for Geoff.

"Corinne?" he answered. "What's wrong?" His stomach clenched with an unknown terror.

"Peter," she said. "Something's happened. Listen, Geoff is

alive, but he's been kidnapped and if I don't give myself up to Rossi, they will kill him." She burst into tears. "They're torturing him, Peter. Electrocuting him, beating him up. Oh god."

Peter's tongue felt thick and his mouth filled with bile. Vivian was watching him, but he couldn't speak. His hands shook. Soon Vivian understood, walked over to him, took the phone, and put it on speaker.

"Corinne, whatever you just told Peter turned him pale. Talk to me, maybe I can help."

Corinne repeated what she told Peter and he realized it wasn't a horrible dream like he hoped. His body ached with a memory.

The pain. The current coursing through his body. The knife being dragged across his stomach and back, never enough to kill, only enough to hurt and maim. The humming sound of the electricity as they switched it on or turned it up. The smell of his chest hair burning off. The booming sound of missiles connecting with their target outside the stone walls. The gunfire. The shouting. His captors grabbing their weapons and racing out the door. The immediate popping sound from a military grade weapon and then the door opening again. The unusual fatigues. The five men who cased the area. The sheer relief and love he felt for whoever it was storming the compound. The man who rushed to him, wearing the Union Jack flag on his uniform. The man flipped his night vision lenses up and lifted Peter's chin. Gunmetal grey eyes, set in a square face, trimmed with mahogany colored eyebrows and lashes met his.

"Stay with me, soldier," the man said, an English accent coloring his words. "We got you." The firefight going on outside was drowned out but when Peter was released from the chains holding him up, his arms having long since lost feeling, he heard a crack in his shoulder, but couldn't feel anything. Good thing too.

He found out afterward his scapula had dislocated. "Stay with me, ranger." He heard the man say in his ear as he draped his arm over the man's shoulders. He shouted something to the men around them, but Peter's ears rang so badly he couldn't hear. "Walk with me, Carlisle. Come on." Peter tried, he tried to put one foot in front of the other, but the numbness in his body overpowered him and he nearly went down, taking the British soldier with him. "Dammit." The man muttered and turned, grabbing his gun, shooting something.

"Don't, please don't leave me," Peter grabbed at him, begging.

"I'm not leaving you, Carlisle. I won't. Promise."

Peter nodded but pain started to assault his body. "Come on. Let's go. Help me!"

Another man raced back and helped lift Peter. The first man bent, and Peter was draped over his shoulder. They ran out of the compound, explosions, shouting, and gunfire all around him. His ribs aching with every pound of his savior's feet, but he was free, and he would be safe. He only wished he knew the man's name.

"Lieu! What have we got?" Another voice said, but Peter couldn't open his eyes. Only when he felt his body be laid out on a flat surface and the heat of the man leave, did he moan.

"Please, wait. Don't leave."

"Easy, Carlisle." He heard the soft voice say in his ear. "I'm here. I'll not leave you."

Then a shot rang out and he felt the heat and spray of blood across his face.

"Lieutenant!" someone shouted as he felt the man's body fall across his.

"I'm all right. Get us the hell out of here, dammit." He rolled off him as another man grabbed his chin and forced him to look at him.

"Did we get him? He's not wearing his dog tags."

"We got him," the same English accented voice grunted.

"Happy Independence Day, Yank," the other man said.

Another soldier with the typical white sash with red cross arm band took over as the truck barreled down.

"I'm fine, dammit, look after Carlisle," the man said.

"You're bleeding, lieu."

"And he's been tortured. I can handle it. Go."

The medic paused a moment then nodded once and turned to him. "What's your name, soldier?"

"Carlisle, my name is... Peter Carlisle." He breathed as the darkness took over.

"Peter. Peter." Someone's hand waved in front of his face and he heard two snaps. "Peter." It was Vivian. "Are you with me? Focus on me."

He shook himself out of his memories and looked at her. Nodding once, he focused on the voices on the phone.

"Can you repeat that, Corinne?" Vivian asked eyeing him. Vivian was always so good with his bouts of PTSD. As a rehabilitation nurse, she had seen her fair share. She was almost as good at Geoff when Peter woke up screaming. Shaking his head, he cleared it again.

"Peter, do you know what, if anything, Geoff could mean by saying he was sorry, and he never forgot Afghanistan. He never told you he loved you and wished you had a chance to be more than friends?" Corinne asked.

Peter's cheeks heated. "What were his specific words?" Peter asked.

"He said all those sleepless nights you just talked about everything, likes, dislikes," Corinne went on.

"He also said how he always made fun of your favorite thing," Lachlan interjected.

"Right, he also said something about it being the anniversary, but didn't say of what," Corinne stated.

Was it? Peter wondered. *How could I have forgotten?*

"Six and a half years ago, I was a POW and Geoff was the one who saved me. He and his squad," Peter explained.

"When?"

"It was... July Fourth," he said.

"I thought he was discharged on Halloween."

"We were, but the uh... anniversary of me being rescued was July Fourth. Why did he say it was today?" Peter questioned.

"Because it's a message," Vivian replied. Not surprising she would think that since her father was a former commander in the Military Intelligence Corps. "Think, Peter. What does it mean? May, something more than friends, favorite thing he used to make fun of, anniversary. Think."

Peter closed his eyes, blocking out the vision of what Geoff must look like being tortured. "May, favorite thing, anniversary, friends... oh dear god. Football." He looked at Vivian. "Two years before I met you, Geoff and I were... ehm... I was living in London and just before Halloween, he told me he had bought me a remembrance gift. It's something we did every year on the anniversary of us getting out. It was tickets to the Champions League Final in Germany. It was between Italy and Arsenal. I was a fan of Italy, he of Arsenal."

"Okay, so how does that help us?" she questioned.

"He always used to make fun of Italy. Saying a good British team was always better. It was all in good fun, but he would do it every chance he got. Anyway, he demanded to go to Arsenals' former stadium as his part of our remembrance. He thought the spirits of past wins there would help his team. It didn't. Italy beat them two to one. But there's an old abandoned football stadium in South-East London known as Invicta Ground. We went together. There are houses all around it now. Not much more than a few steps and a wall. But there was one house, empty and for sale that abutted the wall. He snuck into the cellar to see the original foundations. Nearly got arrested. The Championship game was in May."

"Found it," Lachlan said. "Invicta Ground. I have the address. Peter, how quickly do you think you can get to London?"

"Uhm…"

Vivian beat him to it. "There's an American Flight that leaves at three oh five today. Connecting flight in Philly. Lands in Heathrow at nine twenty tomorrow morning. He'll be on it." Vivian was typing on her phone.

"We'll meet you there. We have two days before Corinne meets Rossi," Lachlan explained.

"Honey, tell me you aren't considering giving yourself up," Vivian said.

"To save Geoff and my father. Yes."

Vivian looked over at Peter urging him to say something. "I'll be there tomorrow, let's talk about this," Peter said.

"Don't worry," Lachlan stated. "It's not going to happen. She'll be safe. I swear it."

"Good," Peter replied. "I'll call when I land."

"We'll get him back, right?" Corinne questioned. "Seeing him being electrocuted... I can't..."

Peter broke out in a cold sweat as memories again resurfaced. "You'll get him." He heard Vivian say. "We got to go. Peter needs to pack a bag."

"Thank you, Vivian," Lachlan said. "I know it's been difficult."

"It's fine, now," she replied. "Talk soon."

They hung up and Peter looked up into Vivian's eyes.

"Breathe..." she encouraged. He did, deeply. "Good. Now, go shower, and throw some clothes into your duffle. I'll make you some breakfast and drive you down to the airport in a couple hours."

"I don't deserve either of that."

"No, but it's what I want to do."

Peter said nothing more. He stared at Vivian's back for a long while after she turned and headed into the kitchen. She grabbed the bread and opened the refrigerator taking out the smoked ham, Gouda cheese and eggs they bought the night before. Then, he took a deep breath. It was going to be the last time he saw her in their kitchen. The last time anything domestic would ever happen between them. He wasn't a misogynistic man, he loved being in the kitchen as much as she did but as she worked, whipping the eggs and cutting the ham and cheese for an omelet or scrambled eggs, he took one long look. It was over. They were done. And nothing would ever be the same again.

Chapter Thirty-One

Lachlan knocked on his parent's door and squeezed Corinne's hand. They had hung up with Peter earlier that day and after Lachlan forced her to eat something, he called his mother asking for a family meeting.

"Are you sure about this, Lach?" Corinne asked.

"Yes, absolutely," he answered with no trace of concern. "My father's and uncles' cousin is deputy mayor and his son is a Garda officer. He'll know what to do."

"But they don't know me."

"Yes, they do," he replied. "And they know me. You are an

O'Quinn. That's what matters."

"But bringing everyone together for me? Rossi is dangerous. I can't let anyone else get hurt."

"And I can't let you go to him," Lachlan said.

Just then, the door opened, and his mother ushered them inside. Everyone stood in the living room. From his uncles to his cousins to his brother, mother, sisters, his Aunt Keera, Uncle Paddy and Paddy's Uncle Tully and Keera's mother Siobhan, and his sister held a tablet connected to a video call with Trevor and Cassie. They all had gathered.

He heard Corinne gasp softly and followed her gaze to his aunt. Keera O'Shea stood next to TS Jameson or Uncle Tully, as he knew him and smiled at her, both world renowned authors and Corinne's favorites. Lachlan squeezed her hand once more before dropping it and stepping forward.

"Thank you all for coming on such short notice," Lachlan began.

"Rachael said it was an O'Quinn family emergency, lad. Of course, we're going to be here," his Uncle Emmet stated.

"Aye, and I'm grateful. For those of you who don't know her," he looked back at Corinne. "This is Corinne McDonnagh." She stepped forward, side by side with him. He half expected his brother to catcall but oddly even Oisín was stoic standing beside his sisters. "She blew into my life and took my breath away. The last ten years have not been easy for me, as you all know but Corinne... she's made me happy again. But she's not safe. The reason I called this meeting is so I can ask for help.

"Corinne came to Ireland on the advice of her best friend, Geoffrey; he is Peter's best friend. She was running from her father's debts. Unfortunately, her father is a degenerate gambler and fell into the wrong crowd. His last bet was against a man named Anthony Rossi, the son of the Rossi family and heir to the *family business.*"

"Are we talking *Godfather*, here?" Oisín clarified.

"We are," Lachlan confirmed.

Everyone's eyes grew wide and Lachlan felt the collective deep breath.

"Go on, lad," his father encouraged.

Lachlan nodded once and took Corinne's hand. "Her da' didn't have any money to gamble with. He only had one thing Rossi wanted."

"Oh jaysus," Siobhan, Keera's mother breathed.

"He waged Corinne in marriage to Rossi... and lost," Lachlan explained. The woman gasped and the men shook their heads in disbelief. "Now, Rossi wants her and has kidnapped Geoffrey. He is torturing him to get her to give herself up. We've spoken with Peter as we were given a message for him from Geoff when the kidnappers called earlier. Peter thinks he knows where he is being held but that's not enough. We have two days before Corinne is expected to meet with Rossi and give herself up in exchange for Geoff's life. I will not let that happen, but I am only one man. I don't have enough power to outwit and outsmart the mafia. That's why I've come to you. I know it's a lot, I know I don't deserve any help but I'm begging you... She means everything to me."

They were silent for a moment until his father stepped forward. "No man has the right to take a woman or anyone, against their will. Just because his father has an army of murderers at his fingertips doesn't mean he's invincible. This Rossi crossed the wrong family. You never have to beg, son. You do deserve our help. We love you. And I've seen firsthand how Corinne has changed you, helped you. She is one of us because of her love for you. For what my help is worth, it's yours."

One by one each of his family agreed. He glanced over at Corinne to see tears in her eyes.

"But what can we do?" His cousin, Aiofe asked from beside her father Emmet.

"I was hoping you could speak with your cousin, Uncle Em? The one who was deputy mayor? He may have some ideas and contacts."

Emmet nodded. "You're going to need the police. Someone to convince them of what's going on. We need a plan."

"And a getaway driver," Killian, Emmet's second born and twin brother to Aiofe, stepped forward.

"No, Killian," Emmet said.

He turned to Emmet; his brows furrowed. "Who here can drive like I can, Da'? No one. I'm the best driver and I can fix on the fly. You know it."

Unconsciously, Emmet's hand drifted to his chest. Lachlan had seen him do that before. The two bullets that nearly killed him twenty-five years ago had long since been removed but the pain and memory of it lingered.

"I'll be fine," Killian winked.

"We'll be on the next flight out," Lachlan heard his cousin Trevor say. "We may not make it before the drop, but we'll at least be there afterward."

"I can talk to our security team," TS Jameson; Uncle Tully, said. "They have connections and can be with you. Let's make a plan, lad."

Everyone except Rachael and Mara, Emmet's wife sat

down. The women went into the kitchen to pull out the sandwiches, tea, and snacks they had prepared. Lachlan watched his family as they all offered ideas. A hand slipped into his and he looked over. His eldest sister Fiona, three years younger than he was, stood by his side. He felt the cold metal of her engagement ring and smiled.

"I'm sorry, Fee," he said.

She looked over at him. "For what?"

He lifted her hand and kissed her fingers. "For not being there for you the last few years. For being a shitty older brother to you. I was too far into my own grief and I cut everyone off. I should never have cut you off too."

She smiled softly at him and cupped his jaw. "Lach, you had every right to be the way you were. You went through hell. I'm sorry I didn't reach out even after you told me not to. But now, she's good for you. I've seen a difference in you just this past hour. But she hurts you, she doesn't know what I'm capable of."

Lachlan chuckled. "I know, love. And I hope Neil knows to treat you right."

Fiona smiled lovingly and looked over at her fiancé grabbing a sandwich and talking with their dad.

"He does."

"Good," Lachlan replied. "I promise, it will be different now."

Fiona nodded and squeezed his hand. "When this is all over, come for a visit. Neil and I would love to have you and Corinne stay for the weekend. Galway isn't that far."

"No, it's not," Lachlan looked over at Corinne sitting with his other sister. "I know it would be wonderful to get away, but I just worry."

"Don't worry," Fiona said. "You got us now. It'll be all right. And Corinne doesn't strike me as a weak woman."

"No," a smile lifted the corner of his lips. "She's not. She's strong and amazing."

"You love her."

"I do," he answered. "I do love her."

"I'm so glad," Fiona hugged him. "No matter what, we're with you. It'll be all right."

"Lachlan, Fiona, loves, come over here and have some tea," their mother called.

They smiled at her, but Fiona squeezed his hand once more.

"We can get through this."

Lachlan nodded and let her hand go. He watched as she headed to the table to get a sandwich and a cup of tea. Her fiancé Neil walked over to her, his hand resting on the small of her back, his thumb drawing small circles. He watched them for a moment, then turned to find Corinne looking at him. Her lips drew up in a smile and he felt a tug at his heart. Yes, everything would be all right. He would make sure of it. He couldn't lose her.

Chapter Thirty-Two

Geoff's entire body hurt. Not just ached like it had after bootcamp but truly hurt. Any movement from sitting up, to moving a finger washed his body in pain. He didn't know how long he had been there. He didn't know what day it was. All he knew was, he had to keep Corinne safe. Praying for the first time in a while, he hoped they had spoken to Peter and he had remembered the tickets he had gotten them and where they went before the game. His hand slowly reached out and touched the foundation wall of Invicta Ground. He remembered that day. It was a good day. He was fortunate, he scoffed admitting it, but he was fortunate the kidnappers took him where he had history. But if Peter was not contacted, Corinne would give herself up and that was something he could never allow.

A door opened somewhere to his right and light filled the small space. He squinted as his room was flooded with fluorescents, causing his eyes to water. He could hear the clicking of men's dress shoes as someone walked down the hallway. Soon his cellar door swung open and the man named George stood in the doorway. He wasn't one of the ones who followed him and kidnapped him, those were the grunts behind him.

"What do you want?" he demanded. *Damn, even speaking hurt.*

"Some good news," George said, and Geoff's heart began to race. "Your girl came through. She's on her way to meet with Rossi now. I'm sure she'll need proof of life and maybe a little incentive to seal the deal. So, rise and shine, pretty boy, it's time for your close up."

One of the grunts slipped past George and grabbed Geoff under the arms. Pulling him roughly to his feet, the other grunt landed a punch to his solar plexus. For a moment, Geoff couldn't breathe, and his sight went black with pain. Proud he didn't show any sort of weakness, he kept his lips together firmly and braced as best he could for a second punch. The grunt didn't disappoint. The second hit was no better than the first and even though Geoff braced, he still blacked out for a short time. Even the simulated torture he endured when he was chosen for the Special Reconnaissance Group helped but wasn't anything like he went through at the hands of civvies.

Finally, Geoff's chin was forced up and he looked into the man's eyes. George would be considered classically handsome, but in a brutal way. His perfect porcelain features were sharp in that movie star way women seemed to love. But it was the darkness behind those baby blues Geoff saw. George grinned and unbidden goosebumps erupted on Geoff's arms and neck as his hair stood on end. It was like looking into the eyes of a tiger, beautiful but vicious and deadly.

"Pity you'll be leaving us so soon," his smooth voice said. "I would have enjoyed getting to know you better."

"Steady on, love, don't want to make your grunt boys jealous, now do we?" Geoff replied. He heard a growl behind him and the one holding him up squeezed tighter. Pain assaulted him but he didn't cry out. "That all you got?" he tossed to the man behind him. "I felt more from your sister last night."

George chuckled and stroked Geoff's cheek. "Don't worry, you'll feel much more if your girl doesn't come through."

George licked his lips and eyed Geoff like a piece of meat and George was starving. A ploy to make him squirm or scared. It might have worked on someone else, but Geoff had gone through hell to get where he wanted in the military. He had seen and done things that would make George scream in horror. His perusal, though unpleasant, meant nothing and Geoff had learned long ago it was better to keep some energy in reserve in case it was needed at the eleventh hour.

"I'm sure you'll enjoy it," Geoff stated. "Just make sure your grunts have a good view, eh?"

George's grin widened and he shook his head. "I'll be the one with the view, my lord."

"Careful, using my title might turn me on." The more Geoff could keep him talking the more energy he could harness and the more time it gave Corinne to get away or form a plan.

"Oh, you won't be turned on, but something might be and attached to you, if you understand me." George winked and looked at the others. "Bring him to the main room. Hook him up. If his girl doesn't come through, we'll have ourselves a little earl roast."

212

"Marquess," Geoff corrected. "At least get my title right, you uncultured swine."

"Ohhoho," George chuckled, then grabbed his chin. "Be sure to smile for the cameras, my lord."

With that, the grunts dragged him out of the room, down the hall and to the main room where he was again handcuffed to the two chains on either side. The whole electrocution thing was getting old. Geoff felt like a piece of spaghetti strung up to dry, either that or a battered Village People extra for the *YMCA*.

George stood a few feet in front of him, a cell phone in his hand. Geoff's eyes wandered to the two exits as they had done the first week he was there. One was directly ahead, behind George, the other was to his left, both impossible in his current position. His only option was to wait and hope. But as he stared at George who paced and tapped his phone again his hand, Geoff swore he would do everything in his power to save Corinne.

Unsure how long they waited, Geoff's arms had lost feeling and his shoulders were beginning to tingle. Used to that by then, he breathed a sigh of relief when George's phone rang. Looking down, George grinned and answered the video call.

Geoff heard a man's voice he had heard only once before by accident. Grunt One and Two had thought he was unconscious, and George had called. There was only one person it could be; Rossi.

"Our little dear heart here wants to see her little friend before she consents to leave with me."

George looked over and Geoff stared back. He was former SRR, leader of his own squadron, what he was going through at the hands of the thugs around him paled in comparison. Nothing scared him, not even death. At least, not his own. Corinne was his weakness. He loved her like a sister and would do anything to keep her safe.

George walked over then slipped behind him, holding the phone in front of Geoff so he could see the screen. Corinne's gasp haunted him.

"I'm fine, honey. Don't worry," he said. "Don't do this, Corrie, please. Don't."

Grunt One smacked him. He tasted blood.

"No!" Corinne cried. "Don't! Please!"

"It's all right," Geoff spat out the blood and looked back at her. "I'll be all right. I'm going to enjoy getting back in here and killing them all. Don't worry. But don't do this."

She shook her head. "I have to. Geoff, Peter says to tell you he loves you too and he remembered your anniversary. He said he knew something was wrong when you didn't call him to remind him about the whole Germany thing. He also told me to tell you Italy still rules, whatever that means." She stared at him.

The sigh of relief he wanted to issue stayed trapped in his chest. Peter remembered. They knew where he was. Good, he needed an HK417 and a Glock. Glancing at the men around him, he internally shook his head. *Too quick. Where's my utility knife?* He wondered. A couple strategically placed stabs would incapacitate them. Then he could let them bleed out as he attached the current.

"So sweet," he heard George sneer in his ear, and it pulled him from his fantasy.

"You've seen him, now, your choice," Rossi said to Corinne. Geoff heard the telltale buzz of the electricity current and his body cringed.

"Don't, Corinne," he ordered. Again, Grunt One smacked him. *Definitely the utility knife...* he thought and held on to the fantasy image of Grunt One clutching his leg after Geoff sliced through his femoral artery.

"Release him," she demanded. "I'll not do anything or go anywhere until you hold up your end of the bargain."

He loved seeing this new side of her. When they got out of the situation, he wanted to hug her and meet the guy who helped coax this Amazon Warrior Woman out of her.

George looked back at Grunt One and Two and nodded. Geoff prepared for the pain and sure enough, when they unhooked him, they let him fall. His numb arms and shoulders were unable to hold him and he heard, rather than felt, a snap. One of his wrist bones had broken and he remembered all those years ago when he heard Peter's scapula had dislocated. His first thought was how was he going to use his knife, but he didn't have to think much longer.

George stood over him, a gun in his hand trained directly at his forehead, the phone's camera aimed at his face.

"Your turn," he heard Rossi say.

A good sweep of his legs and George would be flat on his back, that expense suit dirty on the dusty floor. But then Grunt One and Two would be on him and though he was good, it had been a few years since he left the armed forces and with one arm essentially tied behind his back, he wouldn't be able to take them both. No good plan entered his mind, so he waited.

"Geoff, just go," Corinne cried. "I'm not going to be a problem. Just let him go."

"See... that's the thing, my dear. We already *let him go...* now it's his ability to leave that's questioned," Rossi said.

"Please, just let him go."

There was a pause, then Rossi spoke to George. "Let him go, no guns. He's free to leave."

George stared at him for a long moment, gun still aimed. Then, he tsked and shook his head. "Pity." He lowered the gun and tucked it back into his pants.

"Go, Geoff," Corinne ordered.

"I will find you, I promise," Geoff swore. The throbbing on his broken wrist bone stealing his focus for a moment. Knowing he was on borrowed adrenaline and would soon succumb to the pain, he needed to get out of their clutches and fast. He stood, his legs surprisingly steady. Keeping his eye trained on George, he walked backwards toward the main exit.

George clicked off the phone and never dropped his gaze. A final smirk lifted the corner of George's lips as Geoff walked through the basement door.

Sunlight washed over him and pierced his eyes. The sudden brightness after a month of being in a hell hole hurt, but he took a deep breath of the air and sighed. He was free, but Corinne was not and that thought spurred him on. He needed to find help. Opening his eyes, determined to find a way to save her, he froze and took in the view before him.

Chapter

Thirty-Three

Six Hours Earlier

Lachlan stood with Corinne and Peter in the entryway of Highbourne House waiting on the servant to announce them to the Duke and Duchess of Torrington. The two-day deadline was fast approaching and thanks to his Uncle Emmet speaking with his cousin, the deputy mayor, several doors were open to them and he was cautiously optimistic that their hairbrained plan may actually work. Corinne saddled up to him and took his hand in hers. He could feel the nervous tension radiating off her.

"He'll see us," she sounded as if she was trying to convince herself. "He has to see us. It's his son."

"I won't hold my breath," Peter mumbled. They turned to

217

him, and he huffed a sigh. "I know the hell Lord Torrington put Geoff through. I was there when he disowned him."

"And I was there when Lady Torrington begged him to bring Geoff back," Corinne stated.

"I hope you're right," Peter said. "But if Lady Torrington isn't here… I wouldn't bet on his lordship doing anything."

"We can't do this without him," Lachlan said.

"I know."

"For Geoff's sake we need him," Corinne said.

"Then let's hope his lordship is in a particularly amiable mood," Peter stated as the servant returned.

They stopped speaking as he silently glided across the marble floor. He came to a stop in front of Corinne.

"Lord Torrington apologizes but he is unavailable and asks that you call again at a later time," the servant spoke slowly in the usual way Lachlan had heard in movies.

"Later time?" she gasped. "Does he not realize Geoff's life is in danger?"

Apathetically, the servant answered, "I explained everything as you said it to me."

"And his answer had not changed," Peter scoffed.

"Unacceptable," Corinne replied. Then, pushing past him, she hurried up the steps calling for Lord Torrington. The servant rushed after her demanding she leave, and Lachlan and Peter followed close behind.

Corinne opened every door looking for the study. When she finally found Lord Torrington, she stalked in and stood with her arms crossed. The servant, Peter, and Lachlan raced in behind her.

Lord Torrington stood instantly and with his hands on the desk, he glared at Corinne.

"What is the meaning of this?" he demanded.

"I'm sorry, your grace. She pushed past me, and I could not catch up. My apologies, I will remove Ms. McDonnagh," the servant said hurrying to her.

"You should be ashamed of yourself," Corinne exploded. The Duke's face smoothed into a mask of indifference. "You disowned him once and now you may as well pull the trigger on the gun to his head. How dare you! How dare you be so selfish! Geoff is ten times the man you could ever hope to be!" the servant lunged forward and grasped her arm. Pulling her away, they were nearly out the door before Lord Torrington raised his hand and stopped them.

"You seem well versed in my family's debacles... who are you?" he demanded.

She shook herself out of the servant's hold.

"Corinne McDonnagh, I am your son's best friend," she announced. "He needs help and we came to the only person we know who has the connections to help him. If you don't, he will die."

Corinne and Lord Torrington stared at each other for a long moment before the Duke motioned to the two seats in front of him and dismissed the servant.

"You have burst your way into my home," he began. "I assume there's a reason."

He looked at both Corinne and Lachlan before turning his eyes to Peter still standing by the door.

"You," he said to him. "Step forward." Peter did. "You… dated," his mouth skewed when he said that word. "My son for a time."

Peter answered, "we knew each other in Afghanistan and were hospitalized at the same military hospital in Germany."

"Another war monger, Jesus," he replied. "But I remember you."

"I was around," Peter stated.

"Yes, I never did like the American Yanks."

"We're not overly fond of you either… your grace," Peter said.

"Please," Corinne interjected when she saw the duke's face turn red with rage. "We don't have time for this, your grace. Geoff is in grave danger and he could die if we don't act quickly."

"What has he gotten himself into this time?" he huffed and leaned back.

Corinne breathed a sigh of relief and explained everything that had happened up to that point. Lachlan took her hand in his when he heard her voice catch. For all the duke's stiff upper lip, Lachlan was pleased to see some emotion flicker in his eyes for a brief moment when he heard how his son was being tortured.

After Corinne finished, the Duke of Torrington looked at her for a long moment. "Well? What is it you think I can do?"

Lachlan leaned forward. "Your grace, we were hoping you would be able to assist us in speaking with Scotland Yard. My second cousin is Deputy Mayor of County Kerry, but his influence ended once we crossed the Irish Sea. I was hoping you would speak with someone because we have a plan."

"And what is this plan?"

"Geoff let us know where he is being held. He told us something that Peter was able to translate. Corinne is supposed to meet Rossi at Battersea Power Station. We are hoping to have armed police waiting. Corinne will go to Rossi as if fulfilling her part of the deal. Once she is certain Geoff is released, she will give us a signal. We are hoping for another team to be waiting where Geoff is and as soon as we have Corinne's signal, we will confirm with that team. As soon as he is safe, we want to storm both locations. Arrest Rossi, this George person, and as many of Rossi's team as possible."

Lord Torrington looked at Lachlan for a long moment. Eventually, he leaned forward. "So, you are asking for full tactical response on two boroughs, arrests, and a full sting operation to the heart of one of the largest crime families in the world all in... six hours?" he summed up.

Corinne nodded emphatically. The Duke burst out laughing.

"This is madness, sheer and utter madness. You have hardly any proof apart from one phone call and you are asking for me to justify a covert operation spending thousands of taxpayer dollars simply on the word of one individual and the gambling of your maladroit inebriated father. No, Ms. McDonnagh, I am sorry. You'll get no help from me on this. I am saddened for Geoffrey's plight, but I cannot risk complicating this any further. The Rossis would retaliate and up until now we have had no reason to compromise a seemingly white-collar crime family. My best advice would be to pay the man what he is owed and be done. Even if it is five years of your life, you are young. You have your whole life ahead of you." Lachlan stood, rage radiating from every pore. "And as for my son, he knows I will not condone his war mongering but if it did anything, it should have taught him how to get out of something so malignant."

Before Lachlan could do or say anything, Peter marched

over to his grace. His fist flew at the perfect nose hearing the crack and then thump as the Duke of Torrington fell out of his chair and onto the floor. The Duke looked up at the man who punched him to see Peter step back but crouch down.

"You disowned him once, you now condemn him to death. Just think, my lord how much the Daily Mail would love to hear how you not only hate your son for being a decorated war hero, but you have his blood on your hands. Another tidbit they may be interested in, is Geoff is bisexual and I am sure the newspaper would love to hear about how you so dismissively disprove of that lifestyle. Might lose you a few points in the polls for Prime Minister, eh? If you do not help, I will make it my life's mission to tear down the seat of Torrington. Geoff never wanted it anyway."

"I'll sue you for slander," he spat.

"It's only slander if it's false," Peter pulled out his phone. "And I have you on record, your grace."

The Duke of Torrington stared at the small black device in Peter's hand. Corinne held her breath beside Lachlan. The Duke pulled out his handkerchief and pressed it to his bleeding nose. Standing slowly, he looked at Corinne, then Lachlan.

"After I help you, I never want to see any of you again. You will not tell the media anything about my son," he turned scathing eyes to Peter. "We have how long until the meeting?"

"Five and a half hours."

He nodded and picked up his desk phone. They were silent as it rang, then, "Sir Stephen Wallaby please, this is the Duke of Torrington." They waited again, then when someone answered, the Duke spoke in a jovial tone. "Stevie, Bill, how goes it?"

Chapter Thirty-Four

Lachlan watched on the small screen in the tactical van down the road from the meeting point. Corinne was waiting at the agreed upon location. His chest ached. The night before they met with the duke had consisted of dinner with Peter, then a quiet night in their hotel room. Lachlan had played soft music on his phone and ordered a bottle of red wine. They danced a slow song together, drank, held each other, and eventually made love. Just as he was falling asleep, he held her close to him and begged that she would be there when he woke up. Not to leave in the middle of the night to sacrifice herself. He woke to her kissing his jaw, having stayed by his side all night.

Now as he watched her on the grainy feed, he ached to take

her away from all the pain and worry. The double sting operation was well underway. Peter went with the twenty men and women in uniform to save Geoff and Lachlan was on site with the remaining police a block away from Corinne. The Duke of Torrington and Sir Stephen, Deputy Commissioner of Scotland Yard watched at a secure location in HQ.

Corinne looked to her right and Lachlan saw a black limousine pull up just in the view of the camera. The passenger side door opened and a man in all black stepped out and around to one of the backseat doors. A man who fit Corinne's description of Anthony Rossi stepped out.

"Run facial rec on him," the leader of Lachlan's group ordered one of the techs. Lachlan looked at him.

"You don't know what Rossi looks like?"

"Oh, no, I know that's him. He's not shy about his public appearances. But it's protocol," Ground Leader stated.

Lachlan nodded and turned back to the screen when he heard Rossi through Corinne's microphone. "Corinne," he said smoothly. "Glad to see you've come to your senses."

"Release Geoff," Corinne ordered.

Anthony chuckled. "Dear me, you are in no position to make demands."

"George said if I gave myself up to you, Geoff would be released. I will not go with you until I know he is safe."

He stared at her for a long moment. "I thought your defiance would make you irresistible, but truthfully, all it does is irritate me."

"I don't care what it does, I am here. I am willing to fulfill my father's odious bet, but I refuse to go with you until I know Geoff is safe."

Anthony sucked his teeth but eventually nodded. Pulling out his phone, he dialed a number.

After Corinne had spoken with Geoff and tried to tell him Peter knew where he was, she gave the signal to the van watching her. Lachlan looked over to the leader and he radioed to the other team. Lachlan held his breath waiting for confirmation.

It was an agonizing thirty seconds and Lachlan's chest burned. Releasing the breath, he watched Ground Leader. Another thirty seconds went by, then another. Each passing moment, Lachlan's pulse beat faster. Finally, he heard the Bravo Team Leader announce the package was secure and the rush of relief coursed through him, making him lightheaded.

His eyes drifted from Corinne's screen to the one behind him. Seeing Peter and Geoff embrace then be engulfed by the armed police and hurried to the ambulance, he smiled. It was over.

Then, horror, as he turned back to Corinne's screen. Too late to see what had occurred, all he saw was her slipping into the limousine and the door shutting behind her.

"No!" he bellowed. Jumping out of the van, he ran as fast as he could, but he only saw the dust as the limousine drove away and turned a corner.

Panting hard, he shouted; "Corinne!"

He hadn't protected her.

He hadn't saved her.

She was gone.

Chapter
Thirty-Five

Lachlan hadn't moved from the spot where Corinne had just been standing. His heart constricted. *Why had she gone?* They had Geoff. He was safe. *What happened?*

Several of the firearms unit operators rushed up to him. They had been waiting for the order which never came.

"Sir," he heard Ground Leader say as he jogged up to him. Lachlan turned and was handed a phone.

"What?" he took the phone and put it to his ear.

"What the hell happened?" The Duke of Torrington's voice spat over the receiver. "Why did she go with him?"

"I don't know," Lachlan ground out. "Then pulling out his own phone, he breathed a sigh of relief when he saw the find app still tracking her phone. "Oh, thank god," Lachlan breathed. "They're not far. Heading south east on B two-twenty-four. If we hurry, we can catch them."

"No," another voice came over the phone.

"Excuse me?"

"I can't justify the man hours. We have the Marquess. Ms. McDonnagh had her chance. She chose to go with him. We cannot spend the manpower. This is over. Place Ground Leader on the phone."

"Sir Stephen, no, please."

"Now, Mr. O'Quinn. Stand down."

"No, I will not."

"Now, Mr. O'Quinn, remember you are on my territory. You are not in Ireland anymore," Sir Stephen stated.

Lachlan knew in that moment he would not be taken seriously by Sir Stephen Wallaby. Instead, other people came to mind. The longer he thought about it, the more he realized it would have to be them. Handing the phone to the ground leader, he pulled up his text app and sent the text he hoped never to send.

Lachlan: Secondary plan is a go.

Sending the text to all O'Quinns, he flipped back over to Peter's text chain.

Lachlan: How is he?

Peter: He's worried about Corinne but they're running tests. He's dehydrated, malnourished, and exhausted. We won't know the extent of his internal injuries until they run tests at the emergency room.

Lachlan: Good. As expected, we got the stand down order. Killian should be here any minute.

Peter: Be careful. Find her. Keep me posted.

Lachlan: Will do.

He watched as the armed police headed out. The ground leader walked up to him.

"Sorry, sir, I've been asked to not let you out of my sight," he said.

Anger bubbled to the surface and Lachlan felt his former self coming out. Burying emotions, he felt empty. *Good,* he thought. *It will help.* Catching Killian's car glint in the sun, slowly easing through the armed police, Lachlan nodded to the ground leader.

"Of course," he agreed. "If babysitting a grown man is in your job description, fine. But I would not want to be that person. Besides there's not much more I can do here. I'll be on my way."

The ground leader said nothing, and Lachlan watched his cousin, driving one of Uncle Emmet's sporty cars, come closer and closer.

"Unfortunately, I was told to take you down to Scotland Yard. They don't trust you not to go off on your own."

That angered Lachlan even more, but he embraced the dead feeling inside and stayed where he was. One of the officers called to Ground Leader, and Lachlan took his chance as he turned away. Moving as fast as he could, he slipped into the passenger side of Killian's car, grabbed his seatbelt and, "drive," he ordered.

Killian grinned, slammed the gearshift, popped the clutch, and peeled away. Ground Leader's bellow was drowned out by the screeching tires. Lachlan looked in the rearview mirror seeing Ground Leader gesticulate wildly toward his men ordering them to follow, but Killian was right, no one could drive like him and soon they left the armed police in the dust.

"Whoo!" Killian let out a whoop of excitement. His wide smile lit his eyes and Lachlan laughed

"Damn, Kill," he said. "Where did you learn to drive like this?"

A mischievous glint entered his eyes and slant of his grin. "Can you keep a secret?"

"Of course."

"Uncle Tom taught me," he explained, speaking of his mother's sister's husband and his father's best friend. "He and Da' used to do drag races. Da' doesn't want Aoife to know, but he told me."

Lachlan laughed. He could see his Uncle Emmet doing drag races, he was a daredevil in his youth. He could also see him hating the idea of his son doing it too. Turning his attention to his phone, he watched as the little blue dot slowed.

"Looks like they're stopping," he said.

Killian pressed a button on the steering wheel and after the disembodied voice asked for a command, Lachlan waited as the phone rang.

"Hello?" His Uncle Emmet's voice said.

"Da', I just wanted to let you know, I'm claiming this car as part of my promotion gift."

"Oh, are you now?" Emmet asked a teasing edge to his voice.

"Yep, just thought you should know. It's mine now."

"Uh huh," Emmet replied, and they heard the smile in his voice. "We'll discuss this later. Are you lads all right?"

"Aye," Killian grinned. "I got him. We lost the cops."

"Don't sound too pleased about that, lad." Though it was a reprimand, both Lachlan and Killian heard the pride in his voice. "But good. I got you on speaker. We see the ping, Lach. Fiona has mirrored your screen and we see what you see."

"It's actually a clone, Uncle Em," Lachlan's tech genius sister said.

"Whatever it is, you know I'm lost in technology after about fifteen years ago," Emmet replied.

"But we still love you," Fiona teased back. "Lach," his sister said. "I'm triangulating her position. You used the app I downloaded, right? Not the one that comes with the phone."

"Right," Lachlan said.

"Good, it's more secure and accurate," Fiona went silent for a second and they heard her typing.

Lachlan's stomach was in knots. He swore to Corinne that morning he wouldn't let anything bad happen and now his worst fear was coming true. The clicking of the keys on the keyboard stopped abruptly and Lachlan checked the connection.

"Fee?" he asked. There was nothing on the other end. "Did we lose you?"

"No," she finally answered, but the tone in her voice made his palms sweat. "Lach," she went on. "They've stopped and the only thing around there is St. Mary's of the Immaculate Heart Catholic Church."

Black specks entered his vision and he felt sick.

"The bastard is going to force to her to marry him," Killian's voice was low.

"I'll call—" Emmet's voice drifted in and out of Lachlan's ringing ears.

He didn't hear Killian hang up but soon they pulled into a nearly empty lot two blocks away from the church. Lachlan's ringing ears heard the bells sound the bottom of the hour. Taking a deep breath, he had allowed the fear to run over him for too long. He needed to be fully conscious of what was happening if he had a chance of knowing what to do when the time came. Drawing on his *doctor mode* as Corinne always teased him, he pushed his emotions aside. Getting out of the car, he walked over to the ten men gathered in the parking lot.

Oisín, his father Cabhan, his uncles Emmet, Innis, Sean, Paddy, and Tom along with his cousins, Liam, Egan, and even Trevor, looking tired but there, all waited by their cars.

"I won't ask how you all got her so quickly, but I will say, thank you. Corinne means everything to me. I didn't believe in a second chance until her. I can't lose her. To know my family stands with me, means the world to me."

"Then let's get her back, lad," his father said.

"It's not going to be safe," he answered. "These are dangerous men, if you want to back out, I understand."

"No backing out," Oisín stated after no one spoke or moved. "Let's go get your woman."

He smiled at his brother and nodded. "Let's go."

Chapter

Thirty-Six

All Corinne could do was hope and pray Lachlan wasn't too far behind them. As soon as Geoff was safe, Anthony showed her a picture of her father, bloody and beaten and being held at gun point. As much as she hated what he had done to her, she couldn't let him die.

Anthony's stipulation to let him go was to get into the limousine and go to a church. She knew what that meant... marry him. Bile rose in her throat. She sat as close to the door as physically possible, but Rossi slid closer to her. He slipped some hair behind her ear and moved her chin to look at him.

"So lovely," he said. She suppressed her shudder as he

licked his lips. "When your father made the bet, I could scarcely believe my good fortune and when he told me I would be your first? Heh, I was amazed. I had to do anything to win that hand. It wasn't easy, but here we are."

Corinne prevented her reply. It was something she wouldn't reveal yet.

"Nothing to say?" he asked. "It's all right. No need to be nervous. I hope you know; I didn't want to do any of this to get you to join me, but a bet is a bet. And I'm a man of honor. It needed to be filled. Now, once we are joined in marriage, I'll release your father and we will go to my penthouse. It's been made ready for us."

Corinne said nothing, worried she would reveal something. Her only hope was to either get out on her own, she looked at the two men in the front seat and the two others sitting on the farthest side of the limo, *not likely,* she thought. Her other option was Lachlan. Still, she formulated a plan. If she could get her hands on a knife or even a pair of scissors, she could defend herself against his advances. She knew human anatomy from her independent studies as a Vet Tech. She could incapacitate and even kill if needed. Her phone burned in her pocket and she said a silent prayer hoping the tracking app Lachlan's sister Fiona had downloaded the night before worked.

The limo slowed and came to a stop. Anthony waited until one of the men upfront came around to open the door for him. The two bodyguards slipped closer and all four of them got out. Rossi wrapped his arm around her waist, not out of affection. Corinne was fairly certain it was to prevent her from bolting.

She looked around the area, it was a bustling borough and before her was an intimidating Gothic church. She tamped down her fight or flight feeling and walked into the church.

Her body tingled when she looked down the long aisle to

see her father on his knees, one eye swollen shut, a cut on his cheek, and another on his eyebrow. A man she had never seen before, held a gun to his head. He looked up at her and his one eye grew wide. As much as she tried, she couldn't find any feelings for him. He had caused so much evil to enter her life and now she was supposed to give herself away to the man beside her.

She looked away and locked eyes with a priest. He was dressed in a white robe and held a Bible in his hands. The uncanny similarity in features to Rossi cemented her thoughts they were related.

"Antony," he said, and Corinne heard the remarkable accent and lack of the *th* in his name. "And this must be your lovely bride."

"Indeed, Uncle, this is Corinne McDonnagh."

"Beautiful," he said. The bells rang the bottom of the hour. "Ah, let's begin."

"No!" Her father shouted just before he was struck by the man behind him. He whimpered and looked over at Corinne.

She locked eyes with her father. "Just remember," she began. "This is all your fault. Mum, this, everything."

"I'm sorry," his voice cracked.

"Let's begin," Anthony said. "I'm eager to show my bride all I have in store for her."

The priest chuckled ominously, and Corinne fought the shiver that raced up her spine.

"Dearly beloved," the priest began with the traditional opening. "We are gathered here in the sight of God and in the face of these witnesses to join together this man and this woman in holy matrimony. This wonderful union is not to be entered in lightly but reverently, passionately, and solemnly. If any person can show just cause why these two should not be joined, speak now or forever hold their peace."

At that moment, the door burst open and Corinne looked over. Oisín had kicked the barred door open and stepped aside. Lachlan, in all his brilliance, dark brown hair and toffee colored eyes, walked in, followed by ten other men all of whom she recognized from two days ago at the O'Quinn family meeting.

"Sorry to interrupt," Lachlan said. "But that's my woman you're trying to steal."

She smiled widely at him, then turned to look at Anthony.

"Oh, and I suppose I forgot to mention, I already gave my first time to the man I love." She relished the look on his face as she raced down the steps and into Lachlan's tight embrace. For a second, he held her then pushed her behind him. His father stood behind her, cloaking her in their protection.

"It's over, Rossi," Lachlan said.

"Guards!" Anthony shouted.

"Oh, you mean the three weaklings you left outside?" Oisín asked and flexed his arms in front of him. "Yeah," he breathed. "They may need a hospital."

Rossi looked at the man holding her father. "Kill him!"

"I wouldn't do that if I were you," Lachlan said and once certain the gun wouldn't be used, he looked over at Trevor who had his phone out and pointed to him.

"This is a live stream to everyone I know and I'm sure the police would enjoy it," Trevor said. "Say hello to the world, Crime Boss, murderer, and would-be rapist Anthony Rossi."

"You have only one choice, Rossi," Lachlan spoke again. "Give yourself up."

He scoffed. "Do you have any idea who I am?"

"Yes," Lachlan answered. "That's the point."

"Drop your weapon!" a foreign voice shouted at the front of the church. The sanctuary was stormed by police. The O'Quinn men parted and let the police through. The man she had met once earlier that day who oversaw the ground operations jogged up to Lachlan.

"Dammit, man, if you had waited one more second, you would have heard me say I was ordered to not let you out of my sight *but* they didn't specify where we go *before* Scotland Yard. I was just about to tell my team to follow when that boy raced off like some Indy 500 driver." He glared at Killian.

"Sorry about that," Killian said looking sheepish.

"I don't understand?" Lachlan replied.

Ground Leader huffed a sigh. "I've been after Rossi for years and wasn't about to let him go. Especially not with a woman involved."

"Sorry," Lachlan answered. "I didn't know who to trust."

"Well, now you do," Ground Leader said. "Sometimes it's okay to bend the rules of those who don't understand. Sir Stephen meant nothing by it."

Lachlan nodded but wrapped his arm around Corinne. She rested her head on his chest as they watched Rossi and his man being handcuffed and led out of the church.

"I knew you'd come for me," she said turning her head to rest her forehead on his chest.

Lachlan tightened his hold. "Always, love. I love you. But don't ever scare me like that again."

"I love you, too," she went up on her toes to kiss him. Once their lips touched, she melted. He was her home. But then Geoff came to her mind and she pulled back, guilt descending for not thinking about him sooner. "Geoff?"

"Safe and sound," he answered. "Peter is with him. He's dehydrated and malnourished but so far, he's okay. At last report, they got George and the two henchmen who held him."

"Oh, thank God!" she cried and threw her arms around his neck. He lifted her up and held her tightly. She squealed. "Can we go see him?"

"Of course, but after that, I'm taking you home."

"Home," she sighed. "Aye, take me home, O'Quinn."

Lachlan grinned and leaned down to kiss her. Before either of them got carried away, her father hobbled over, and they turned to look at him.

"Corrie," he sobbed. "I'm sorry. I'm going to get help. I promise. No more drinking, no more gambling. I'm sorry."

Corinne shook her head. "No, you do whatever you want. I can't do this with you anymore."

"Corrie," he gasped. She was happy Lachlan stayed quiet.

"No dad, I can't trust you. I can't forget. I forgive you, but I will not put myself, Lachlan, his family, or any children I may want or have at risk simply by knowing you. I hope you get help. I hope you get sober. But I will not be around to see it. I'm sorry it's come to this, but you have hurt me once too many times. Goodbye, dad. I wish you nothing but happiness and love."

She turned to go, Lachlan holding her to his side. She felt a weight lift from her shoulders. As soon as they were outside, she watched Rossi, the priest, and the man who held a gun to her father be walked into the police transport and the three men who rode in the limo with them, were being dragged into the van too. Clearly Oisín had knocked them out. On the steps of the church, Lachlan turned to her and held her in his arms, there was nowhere else she'd rather be. The soft thump of his heart beating beneath his brown sweater soothed hers and soon they were breathing as one.

"I thought I lost you," he whispered.

"Never," she answered and pulled a little away from him, their arms still around each other. "I knew you'd come, and I only had to delay them."

"It's over, love. You never have to worry about this ever again."

"I know," she said. "Thanks to you and your family."

"*Our* family, love," he stated. "And honestly, I for one am glad all this happened. It brought you into my life. You helped me live again, love again. I only hope one day I can repay you for everything you've done for me."

Corinne grinned and slipped her fingers through his. "I'm sure I'll think of something."

Lachlan laughed and leaned down. "I look forward to it," he breathed just before he pressed his lips to hers.

Chapter Thirty-Seven

His body ached. Not as badly as it had in the past, but still, ached. He heard a soft beeping and filled his lungs as much as he could. Disinfectant, mixed with bergamot, sage, and pine. Peter's cologne "Geoff?" he heard the familiar voice say. Slowly, he opened his eyes to see Peter leaning over him and tried to smile.

"Hey," he said softly. He tried to sit up but grunted as pain assaulted his every pore. It took the breath out of him and he fell back on the hospital bed panting. Peter immediately wrapped his arms around him to help. But that put them too close. Geoff looked up at him, startled at how near his face was. He could see the green flecks in Peter's blue eyes and feel his breath on his cheek.

"Easy," Peter breathed. Geoff nodded and was finally able to sit up. Peter, almost like a mother hen, fluffed the pillows behind him and guided him with his strong hand on the back of Geoff's neck.

"Thank you," Geoff said. "How long was I out?"

"A couple hours. But I knew you'd want to know. Corinne is safe."

Geoff sagged against the bed in relief. "Thank God. What happened?"

"Lachlan convinced the O'Quinns to help and then convinced Scotland Yard. It was a massive sting operation."

"I saw that," Geoff replied with a slight smile. "And Corinne is safe?"

"Safe with Lachlan. They're on their way here."

"Good. What about George and Grunt One and Two? Were they captured?"

"Grunt One and Two?" Peter chuckled. "Very descriptive, my lord. But yes, they're being held."

"Good, I need my utility knife and five minutes alone with them."

Peter chuckled. "You know that is not going to happen."

"A man can dream." Then, looking over at Peter, he stared at him for a long moment. "I'm sorry," he finally said.

Peter's brows furrowed. "For what?"

"For leaving you in that hell hole for that long. I can only imagine what you went through."

Peter's face paled but he shook his head. "You didn't know

me then. If it weren't for you checking the underground bunker, I would have died in there."

"Never," Geoff stated taking his hand. Peter looked down as if surprised he made the move.

"Geoff," Peter began and when he looked up, Geoff saw what he was going to say. Removing his hand quickly, he clasped them in his lap.

"How's Vivian?" Geoff questioned.

Peter breathed out through puffed cheeks. "Free," he answered. "We broke up."

"I'm sorry," Geoff said though the relief that spread through him was dizzying. Peter searched his face, his eyes impassive.

"No, you're not," he said.

Geoff took another deep breath. "You're right. I'm not. I never did like her. She wasn't good enough for you. But I am sorry."

"It's fine. I am glad in a way."

"She didn't want you to come here? To be with me?" Geoff asked.

Peter paused a moment and Geoff had his answer. "She knows... about what happened in Germany. I had to tell her."

"And that broke you up?" Geoff wasn't as surprised as he sounded.

"In a way..." Peter admitted. "She knew I had never fully... gotten over what happened... between us."

Geoff nodded slowly. "I know. Me neither. But that was then, this is now."

Peter looked away. "I'm glad I'm able to be here with you."

"I'm glad you understood my message."

Peter looked uncomfortable about something. Geoff had always been able to read him like a book. He was hiding something. "What is it?"

"Uhm..." Peter started. "Your dad knows..."

"What?" Geoff asked, his face stoic but his heart beat faster.

"It was the only way to get him to help. He had the connection with Sir Stephen Wallaby with Scotland Yard we didn't. I... sort of blackmailed him. I said I would go to the media about your... sexuality."

Geoff couldn't breathe. He felt like he was drowning. His father couldn't know. He never intended him to know.

"I'm sorry after I said it, I realized..."

Closing his eyes for a moment, Geoff took another deep breath. "It's all right. It just gives him another reason to hate me."

"I'm so sorry."

Geoff shook his head. "Stop apologizing, Carlisle," he said.

They were quiet for a long moment, Peter looking like a worried little boy. Geoff pushed some overgrown hair out of Peter's eyes and they both froze.

"I—"

"Yes?" Geoff prompted, not dropping his hand.

"I'm sorry I didn't come to find you sooner. I knew something was wrong. I should have... You would have scoured America for me after week two and I was too busy trying to be someone I'm not. I'm sorry."

"No one knew what happened to me," Geoff encouraged cupping his jaw. "Hell, I didn't even know. I was walking home from the pub and got jumped, which is crazy in itself for me. Woke up in that place. I only knew where I was because of the stone stamped with the date and the football motto."

"You were there for a month."

"Is that how long?" he questioned dropping his hand, almost tired after holding it up for a few short moments. "I lost count after the first electrocution."

The moment he said the word, he bit his tongue. *Dammit...* he watched Peter's face go ashen. Geoff topped Peter's hand with his.

"Look at me, Carlisle," Geoff ordered. Peter lifted his eyes to meet his. They stared at each other for a long moment, Peter's breathing finally evened out. "You with me?"

Peter nodded. "Bad memories."

"I know. I'm sorry. It was my memories of you, your courage, bravery, and fortitude that saved me from going mad. England had to save America's arse for once back then," he winked.

Peter laughed and agreed. They both looked toward the door when someone knocked. Geoff removed his hand off Peter's and called, "come in?"

A doctor walked in, carrying a clipboard. "Good afternoon, Lord Garvey," he said using the correct title as befitting Geoff's station as Marquess of Garvey, a lesser title of his father's, the Duke of Torrington. "I am Dr. Gupta, your tending physician. Your blood panels came back normal. I know you experienced electrocution, but you look to be healing with no long term affects.

I'd like to keep you for a couple days for observation, but you should be able to go home by Friday."

"What day is it?"

"Tuesday," Peter provided.

"Thank you," Geoff said.

"I would also recommend you not be alone and light to minimal physical excursion for a couple weeks. No long workouts, walking is permitted but only short distances to build up your strength. I would recommend a heart monitor when needed in order to prevent overuse. Your heart sounded strong, but after what you went through, we want to be careful. Listen to your body. It will tell you if it's ready or not."

"Of course," Geoff agreed.

"As far as foods, nothing fatty and no rich foods or red meats for a time. Also limit alcohol intake. I will give you a list of proper foods and some light exercises. I will also prescribe a mild sedative to help you sleep. I recommend you check in with your general practitioner in a couple weeks. He or she will want to administer a stress test when you are fit enough. If you have any questions, please feel free to call for me or one of the nurses."

"Thank you, doctor," Geoff replied and watched the doctor leave the room.

"I'll stay with you," Peter offered.

"You don't have to."

"I know, but I want to. It might also be good to utilize your cook more now."

"She'll like that. She always hates it when I butt into her kitchen," Geoff chuckled. They were silent for a long moment. "I'm glad you're here, Peter."

Peter smiled slightly. "Nowhere I'd rather be, Geoff."

They took each other's hand and held it until another knock sounded. Dropping Peter's hand, Geoff looked over as the door swung open. Corinne hurried in, followed by Lachlan who Geoff had only seen once before when he went to Ireland with Peter.

"Oh my god! You're alive!" Corinne cried and raced to his bed.

"Hey, honey, I'm fine. Thank god you're all right. That was a foolish thing to do," Geoff stated but hugged her gently, his body still aching.

"You have no idea," Lachlan said.

Geoff looked at him. "Good to see you again, Lachlan. It's been... what, years?"

"Aye, it's good to see you too, Geoff," he said. "I'd offer to shake your hand but..." he gestured to Corinne in the way.

Geoff watched as Peter stood from his seat beside him and walk to Lachlan. They shook hands and embraced as Corinne pulled back and stared at him.

"I couldn't let them hurt you," she justified. "I'm just so glad Peter understood your message. What exactly is your history with each other? You never told me."

"Military," he answered.

"Besides that. There's got to be more."

"We're best friends," Geoff replied.

Corinne looked back at the men behind her and Geoff focused on Lachlan standing a little way away, talking with Peter. He was older than Corinne, but those years looked good on him.

Dark hair with a sprinkle of grey throughout, average height and trim figure, but the eyes were the windows to the soul as his old nanny used to say and Lachlan's eyes showed pain but there was also a great amount of love when he caught Corinne's eye. Geoff approved of the soft smile that rested on his lips and the heat that entered the eyes. Lachlan was good enough for her.

Geoff's eyes moved to Peter standing beside him, the fluorescent lights toyed with his blonde hair making it twinkle like gold. He smiled then laughed at something Lachlan said.

"Oh my god, you love him," Corinne's voice whispered near his ear.

"What?" he turned suddenly to her. Her blue eyes far too knowing. "Don't be ridiculous, honey."

"I've never seen you look at *anyone* like that," she said.

"He's my best friend, any love there, is purely platonic." He was proud at how firm his voice sounded. "You look well. I'm glad you're all right."

"Me too," she answered. "And though your change of subject wasn't at all subtle, my lord, I have you to thank for being so happy."

"Oh?" he smiled.

"If you hadn't told me about Ireland, I would never have met Lachlan."

"I'm glad you met him," he said.

"You approve?" she asked anxiously.

"Does he love you?"

"Yes," she grinned.

"Does he treat you well?"

She nodded. "Extremely."

"Have you two…" He trailed off. She blushed but nodded. "And he respects you? And doesn't hurt you?"

"He absolutely respects me and has never hurt me," she said.

"Good, then yes, I approve," he winked again but suddenly pain gripped his body. He gasped, leaned his head back on the pillows, and groaned.

"Geoff?" he heard Corinne and Peter both say. He felt Peter rush to his other side and grip his hand. Peter's other hand rested on his forehead. "What's wrong?"

"Spasm," Geoff breathed. "Can't breathe."

"Breathe, just breathe, Ainsley," Peter coaxed.

Geoff nodded and after a moment opened his eyes again. "Sorry," he said. "That hurt."

"I understand more than you know," Peter replied stroking his hair back, wiping his sweaty brow.

Geoff looked over at Corinne, tears gathering in her eyes.

"Oh honey, come here, I'm fine." He opened his arms to her, but she shook her head.

"I don't want to hurt you," she sobbed. Lachlan's hands rested on her shoulders, his forefingers slowly rubbing circles on her collar bone.

"You won't. I'm all right. Promise." Again, he reached for her and she hugged him gently.

After a moment, a nurse knocked and opened the door to his hospital room. Only then did he realize he wasn't sharing a room with anyone as was usual.

"Forgive me, Lord Garvey, but your mother and father are here. I've been asked to show them in but first, I must tell you, you need to limit your visitors."

"We'll go," Lachlan offered. "We'll come back tomorrow."

"Right, good," Geoff replied and took Corinne's hand, squeezing. "I can't tell you how much I care about you, Corrie. Thank god you're safe."

"You too," she reached over him and kissed his forehead. "I love you, Geoff. I'll see you tomorrow."

"Love you too, honey," he said. "See you tomorrow."

"Take care," Lachlan called as he ushered Corinne out of the room. The nurse smiled at them, then turned to look at him.

"Ten minutes, my lord. You need your rest," the nurse said and then stepped out of the room.

Geoff took a deep breath preparing for his parents. His mother was first to appear and in true British Aristocracy fashion, her stoic countenance did not change. If Geoff didn't know his mother well, he would have missed her subtle shift. Her eyes were bright with concern and her movements stiff as if holding herself back from rushing to his side.

"Mother," he greeted.

"Geoffrey," she said. "Are you well?"

"Better than I could have been."

His father walked in next and Geoff steeled himself for the disapproving look on his father's face. Sure enough, the Duke's eyes went immediately to Peter standing beside him and the thin purse of his lips showed his displeasure as he looked back at Geoffrey.

"Sir," Geoff acknowledged his father. "I appreciate you coming to see me."

"It was your mother's idea," the Duke stated.

"Still, it is acknowledged and appreciated," Geoff said. He felt the bewildering surprise from Peter beside him but was grateful his best friend stayed silent.

"Peter," Geoff's mother greeted him with slight smile. "It is good to see you, again."

"Your grace," Peter bowed his head slightly. "The pleasure is mine."

His mother finally walked over to his bed and looked down at him. "What did the doctor say?"

"After being cooped up and electrocuted for a month, I am in surprisingly good health," Geoff couldn't prevent the bitterness in his voice. He felt Peter tense but couldn't focus on him.

His mother's gasp and sharp look at his father was at least some sort of reaction. "You did not tell me that, William."

"I did not know, my dear," the term of endearment was more a warning, than a moniker.

"Bullshit," Peter mumbled for only Geoff's ears.

"Did the doctor say if there would be any… lasting affects?" his mother asked turning back to him.

"No, I'm sure I'll still be able to perform my duty and marry Lady Winifred. You will have an heir. *That* at least was not compromised," Geoff said. Peter's deep breath beside him was loud in his ears. It was no secret Geoffrey and Lady Winifred Russell were to be married. Though the announcement had not been made and neither liked the other very much, the aristocracy did it differently. He had a duty, no matter where his heart lay.

"I'm sure she will be very glad to hear it," his mother said. "She called when news of the incident spread. I will be sure to let her know."

"Yes, indeed. Well, I truly appreciate you both coming to check on me. I will be discharged in a couple days. Peter will be staying with me at my townhouse during this time."

His father harrumphed. "I do not believe that is appropriate."

"Why?" Geoff turned hard eyes on him, almost daring him to out him in front of his mother.

"Yes, William, why? Peter and Geoffrey served together. They are great friends." She turned to Peter. "I place my faith in you, Peter to get him back to full strength."

"Of course, your grace," Peter answered.

"I will have my secretary hire a live-in nurse to assist you, Carlisle. I'm sure you are eager to return home to America," the Duke stated.

"No need for that, Father."

"There is need," he replied sternly. "Besides, it shouldn't be for longer than a few weeks. I will call Lady Winifred's father and we will discuss terms."

"How very romantic," Geoff stated dryly.

"Well, then," his mother said nothing more and Geoff almost hated her for it. She always allowed his father to dictate his life. "You get better, dear."

"Yes, mother," he answered. She kissed his forehead and turned to go.

"There is no need for a nurse, William. I am sure Peter will be far more capable," she said as she walked by him.

The Duke huffed. "Very well then, but I intend on paying you for your time, Carlisle."

"No, that won't be necessary," Peter replied resolutely. "What I do for Geoff, I do out of love." The Duke flinched at the word.

"William," the Duchess admonished. "Come now. Take care, dear."

The door closed and they were alone. "Make no mistake," Geoff began. "You will either have a cheque in the mail, or my father will have as many people as he can drop by to make sure we aren't compromising his plans for my merger with Lady Winifred."

"Merger?" Peter asked.

"That's what I said," Geoff agreed.

"You could refuse."

"Could I?" Geoff questioned. "You have no idea what I can and cannot do, Carlisle."

"No, you're right, I don't. But I do know you don't love her. Can't ever love her."

"No, but we aristos don't marry for love. We have affairs for that."

Peter's chuckle at his nonchalance warmed him. They were quiet for a long moment. Geoff turned his hand palm up for Peter. His best friend slipped his hand in his.

"I'm sorry," Geoff said finally. "I know this... us... our past together has compromised your relationship with Vivian. But that's all it can be, Peter. In the past."

"I know," Peter answered. "But you'll always be my best friend."

"And you mine," Geoff replied. His eyes getting heavy with sleep, he stared at Peter. "Be my best man?"

"Thought you'd never ask," Peter answered, and Geoff saw slight wetness gather in the corner of Peter's eyes.

"I'll be able to get through the wedding with you by my side."

Peter said nothing for a long moment. Then, "rest." Was all he said as he began to stand.

Geoff spoke again, "don't... please don't leave me." Geoff tightened his grip on Peter's hand.

Peter took a shuddering breath as he repeated what Geoff had said to him all those years ago, "I'm not leaving you, Ainsley. I won't. Promise."

With those familiar words in his ear, Geoff drifted off to sleep and dreamt of a better world where he didn't have the ties of family to bind him to a future he never wanted.

Epilogue

Two years later

"Love!" Lachlan called to Corinne as he plated the spinach omelet and bacon. "Breakfast is ready. I made your favorite."

She didn't answer. He waited a few seconds and called to her again. She had a rough night, but he had heard her get up and head to the restroom about twenty minutes ago.

He had just set out Oscar's bowl and watched as the dog attacked the food and bits of bacon he had crumbled up. When he heard the bathroom door open, he turned to her. His smile died on his lips when he saw the look on her face.

"What's wrong?" he demanded and rushed to her.

"Lachlan, I need you to be calm."

"What happened?" his blood pressure skyrocketed.

"My water broke," she admitted.

Fear, adrenaline, and panic crashed over him. He felt lightheaded as his legs grew heavy and his stomach pitched.

"Oh god, oh god, oh god, what do we do? What—"

"Lachlan, stop. I need you to be calm. Our baby is coming, we need to go to the hospital."

"Right, yes, okay, okay," his eyes crossed for a second and he weaved on his feet.

"Lach! Don't make me call Oisín," she threatened almost teasingly.

He nodded once as his vision cleared. She took his hands in hers and waited until he looked at her.

"I know you're scared. So am I. But just think, our daughter wants to meet us. She can't wait for her daddy to hold her. So, let's not make her wait too much longer, aye?"

He nodded and some semblance of composure came over him even if his tongue felt thick in his dry mouth.

"All right, let me get the hospital bag and call Ma so she can come get Oscar. Sit for a minute, I'll be right back."

She shook her head. "If I sit, I won't get back up."

"Okay, I'll be two seconds," he raced to the stove and made sure everything was turned off, then flicked on some lights knowing they wouldn't be home any time soon. He then hurried to the extra room they had converted to the nursery.

When Corinne first brought up the idea of trying to start a family, he thought he would rather die than go through that again, but when she told him she had missed her monthly cycle twice, seven months ago, he had her take a test. When it was positive, some of the anxiety he thought he would feel melted away. And when he saw his daughter for the first time on the grainy ultrasound picture, he felt undying love and fierce protection surge through him. Since then, he hadn't allowed himself to think of losing either her or Corinne. As he grabbed the hospital bag from the nursery, he gave in to the fear for only a moment, then put it away and hurried back to his wife.

"Ready to meet our daughter?" he asked.

"Ready," she stroked her stomach. "Our little Joy."

He took her hand and kissed her knuckles. "Thank you, love. Not only have you brought happiness and love into my life, but you have given me such joy. I worried when we decided to try but how you honored my past without jealousy or distress, you truly are the song of my heart's desire. I love you, Corrie." He kissed her lightly. "Now, let's go meet our daughter."

Corinne smiled even as a contraction pulled over her belly and took his hand. They walked out of the house, hearing a chime from Lachlan's phone. A text from his mother, she was on her way to the hospital and Oisín and Cabhan were going to pick up Oscar.

Twelve hours later, his hand aching from Corinne's grip, a squalling, perfect, wiggling little lass was placed into his arms and as he stared, her eyes opened and fixed on him. His heart sang as tears gathered in his eyes.

Corinne beamed through her tiredness and watched as he rocked their Joy gently in his arms, tears of happiness sliding down his cheeks. His eyes glassy but his heart full and overflowing with love for the two women who dragged him back to the land of the living.

For that, he was eternally grateful.

an deireadh

Acknowledgements

Thank you so much for reading Lachlan's and Corinne's story! I hope you enjoyed it! I want to thank my family who have always supported me especially during this difficult 2020 event season! I hope everyone is staying safe and healthy as we all face this together. It has been an *interesting* year so far as we all know, but I am hopeful we can all move on to a better, brighter future! To all my fans, thank you for still supporting me, I know times are difficult, but your love and support mean the world to me!

When I first came up with the title *The Song of Heart's Desire,* I knew I wanted it to be a heavier story than usual and tackle some of the tough topics not fully covered before. Things like loss, addiction, and PTSD. I knew I wanted it to revolve around Lachlan as I had already written his personality when you first meet him grown up in the pub during Trevor's jury *In Dublin Fair City.* But Lachlan was first introduced as a young twelve-year-old in the first book *Love Among the Shamrocks Collection Under the Irish Sky.* But I loved writing him as a grown man as well as revisiting some other characters like Cabhan, Rachael, Mara, and Emmet, and give you a clear picture of Oisín.

Oisín is the subject of the next novel in the series; *Love Among the Shamrocks Collection The Next Generation*, book three *Chasing After Moonbeams* coming mid-2021. The carefree business owner has been discovered by a modeling agency and becomes one of the most sought after male models in the business. He could have anyone he wanted so when American Renovator

Naomi Moon wants nothing to do with him, he's intrigued.

Again, thank you all from the bottom of my heart for all your support! You help make this fun! I miss you all but look forward to seeing everyone again in 2021!

Read on for a sneak peek to *Chasing After Moonbeams*!

love among the shamrocks collection
the next generation
Book Three

Chasing After

Moonbeams

M. KATHERINE CLARK

Chapter One

Meditation had always been a large part of Naomi Moon's life. It always grounded her, centered her. Many people probably thought it silly. She would rise with the sun and meditate out in her small Zen garden, but ever since she was a young girl, her mother taught her to be one with nature and yourself. Now that her mother was gone, it was a way for Naomi to be close to her.

The only music around her was the soft warm breeze of Florida's Emerald coast and the crash of the Gulf of Mexico's waves on the shore. She knew though it was only a matter of time before the hustle and bustle of the tourists and city roared to life. She cherished these moments just before the inevitable.

"Honey! I'm off to – Oh! Sorry," the sound of her father's voice calling from inside their bungalow made her smile. Then his attempt at a whisper followed by the thumps and bangs as he tried to *be quiet*, made her chuckle.

Taking a deep breath, she came out of her meditation, bowed low, her forehead to the floor, and whispered.

"Until next time, mama."

Then standing, she again filled her lungs with the salty, humid air. Her eyes opened to see her mother's name written in the traditional Hawaiian language her mother had instilled in her. "I love you, mama."

Turning to take the three steps up from outside into the kitchen, she saw her father sitting at the island, chewing a toasted bagel. He looked up and smiled.

"Sorry to interrupt, honey," he said.

"No interruption, dad," she answered. Pulling out the box of cereal, she continued. "I was almost finished anyway."

"I know but being married to your mother for twenty years, I know not to interrupt. I had her wrath more than once," he chuckled.

"Loving wrath," Naomi winked.

"True," he replied and tossed back the remaining orange juice in his glass. "I'm glad you continue her tradition, honey. It keeps her alive in our hearts."

"It feels weird not to meditate. It's my time with her," Naomi said putting a slice of bread in the toaster.

"I know, love," he replied, then sighed. "It's hard to believe she's been gone sixteen years."

"It is hard," she agreed pouring the milk.

"You remind me so much of her, Mimi," he smiled. "So beautiful and kind and stubborn."

She laughed. "Can't forget the stubborn."

"Never," he beamed. "She would be so proud of you."

"I do miss her."

"I know. We both do."

They were quiet for a long moment until they both finished their breakfast.

"Well," her father began. "I'm going to check in at the Sanderson's, make sure everything is going well."

"Have they paid for the extra lumber yet?"

"Not yet," he said.

"Dad..."

"I know. I'll talk to them."

"Be sure to. We need that money."

"I know, Mimi. Where will you be today?"

"I'm going to check on the reno at the Emerald Coast Condominium. Then I have the planning meeting with Olivia over lunch," Naomi explained.

"Oh, that's right, that's today?" He said as he shrugged into his paint overalls.

"Yep. The seventeen year high school reunion planning is in full swing."

"Why is this reunion so important?" He asked.

"I have absolutely no clue," she replied. "Liv said something about it being the same amount of years since she graduated as she was when she graduated. Seventeen year olds. God, were we ever that young?"

"You're one to talk, honey," he teased. "Thirty-five isn't bad at all. Just wait until you hit sixty-five. Then talk to me about seventeen."

He grabbed his keys off the peg by the door and headed out.

"It's just odd, you know? You never hear about the odd numbered reunions, just the big ones. Oh, well, have fun. Let me know how the condo's going. Oh! Can you pick up a couple things at Publix tonight? We need a few things for around the house."

"Sure, and I'll swing by Lucky Sam's and get us dinner."

"Delicious, thanks, love," he leaned over and kissed her cheek.

"Bye, dad, be safe."

He trotted down the steps and toward his old 1970s rust colored pickup truck. Naomi waved at him after he finally got it started and pulled out of the driveway. Naomi waved at him after he finally got it started and pulled out of the driveway.

"Good morning, Mrs. Hester," she called to her neighbor as she headed to the mailbox.

"Good morning, dear," the old woman said. "How's things?"

"Things are wonderful as always. And you? Is your granddaughter coming down this summer again?"

"Oh yes, she and her young man will be here in a month or so," Mrs. Hester said. "How about you, dear? Any young man in your life?"

"Oh now," Naomi shook her head. "No *young* man need apply."

Mrs. Hester laughed. "Well, don't put it past them. You know women in their thirties are marrying younger men. They have enough stamina to keep up," she winked.

Naomi chuckled. "I have to get ready for work. I hope you have an amazing day, Mrs. Hester. Weatherman says it'll be perfect to be by the pool today."

"Oh, don't worry, dear. You need to be home by three,

though."

"Oh? Why?" Naomi asked wracking her brain for the reason.

"Maximillian will be here. He's cleaning my pool today."

"Oh, of course," Naomi muttered while forcing a smile.

"Did you know he just broke up with his girlfriend?"

"Imagine that," again Naomi muttered through a smile.

"You know how handsome he is. And he always likes seeing you."

"Well, I will do my best," Naomi lied. Then with a wave and a see you soon, she shut the door and leaned against it.

Blowing out a breath, she huffed. It wasn't as if she didn't like men, it was more everything that went along with them. She couldn't handle another lying, cheater in her love life. Her ex-husband really did a number on her. Mrs. Hester only knew she had a divorce and moved back home. No one except her dad knew the truth. Since Emilio, there hadn't been another she was willing to open up to.

"Enough," she said aloud. Pushing off the door, she headed to her bathroom for a quick shower. Then, changing into her jeans, branded t-shirt, and boots, she locked up the house and headed to her truck.

Chapter Two

Oisín O'Quinn stared into the clicking camera with as sultry a look as he could muster while sand dug into crevices of his body he didn't know existed. The ocean shoot was every model's dream, at least that was what his manager assured him as they flew from New York to Panama City Beach, Florida.

And if he was being honest with himself, it was exciting. The sun shining down on his bare back, the water crashing over his legs, the heat of the warmed sand under his chest, the screaming fans, aye, Oisín was in heaven.

"That's great, Osh," his manager called from under the umbrella chairs, a Bloody Mary at his elbow. "Looks fantastic."

"I would like a few of you coming up out of the water," the photographer who had the ability to make his life hell, said. Oisín smiled at him and turned over, checking that his swim trunks hadn't ridden up too much before he stood.

Grateful he had conditioned his skin to bear the Florida sun, Oisín still winced as he felt the beginnings of sunburn on his right shoulder. The glorious Irish blood pumping through his veins made him proud to be Irish and yet caused far too much maintenance when in the sun.

A few more shots and the photographer called a break.

Sloshing out of the surf, Oisín gratefully took the offered towel and wiped his face and chest, then used it as a shield to cover his shoulders.

"I love you, Oisín!" one in the crowd of screaming fans yelled.

"I want you!" another cried.

"Marry me!"

Oisín chuckled. Fan girls were one of his favorite parts of the job. One-night stands were all any of them were looking for, a boast to their friends back home, and he was perfectly fine with that. It wasn't as if he was going to settle down. He had just turned thirty and his modeling career was in full swing.

Five years ago, he was helping his mates move a man from his Dublin flat to a retirement home after he had fallen once too many times. As owner of the *Rough and Buff* moving company, Oisín oversaw the project with a keen eye. The company was made up of university friends and the only stipulation was they had to be all attractive and willing to wear nothing but a kilt and boots. It was quite the hit with the ladies. But the move five years ago, Oisín remembered vividly. The man was a flamboyant seventy-two-year-old and he kept staring at him. Not that Oisín cared about being looked at, he was used to it and prided himself on his physique. But the man's gaze was not one of interest or even lust, it was curiosity. After the lads had loaded up the truck, Oisín was going through the checklist with the man and after everything was cleared the man turned to him.

"I could make you a star, lad," he said.

"A star?" Oisín had questioned.

"Aye, have you ever considered modeling?"

The question had taken him aback.

"I still have contacts in the industry. You could be the next Mark Vanderloo."

"I don't know who that is."

"Look him up. Then call me," he offered his card. "We're talking New York, LA, Paris, Milan, everywhere a young man like you would love. Think on it."

And Oisín had thought on it. Searching the internet for information well into the small hours of the morning and that next day, he called the man. The rest happened so fast, Oisín could hardly remember but as he sauntered over to the women screaming his name, his feet sinking into the warm white sand, he knew he would never give up that life. He loved it.

After signing breasts and taking selfies, he made it to his agent who was typing on his phone.

"More sunscreen," he snapped his fingers without looking up. Oisín relaxed into the chair under the umbrella. "I have you booked in at seven tomorrow, and we will need to take a helicopter to get to the island. So, I have a five am wakeup call going to your room in the morning."

Oisín nodded, no party that night. "When's my free day?" he asked as one of the crew rubbed sunscreen on his back.

"You get a few weeks off as discussed for vacation but until next week, you're booked. We booked a beach house for when we're done here, so you'll have your pool party."

"The fact you can read my mind is scary."

"Trust me, I know. Fortunately, it's not all the time."

Oisín chuckled then moaned as the woman began massaging his shoulders.

"I'm going to grab a few things from the store tonight then. I'm tired of room service," Oisín said.

"I've never met anyone who has ever said that."

"I know, but I do miss a homecooked meal and since we can't go out…" he pried.

"Not yet," his manager replied. "You know the rules, no beer, no sugar, no bread until the week is over. I'd hate to have to photoshop out a little bloat."

Oisín looked down at the eight protruding muscles on his stomach.

"Does it look like a little bloat is possible?"

"Beer and bread? Anything is possible. But I trust you. Go with your bodyguard after we finish here."

"I'm going for a run and a swim first. Then I'll go," he revealed. "Coming with me, By?"

The stoic man beside him merely nodded once. The bodyguard was an impressive man, standing nearly seven feet tall and larger than Oisín. Byron was a beast. But Oisín enjoyed his company. Both were displaced for a job and he was quiet but interesting.

There were times Oisín sat with him and asked for advice. Byron was ten years older and had lived a life.

"When you're ready, Oisín," the photographer called.

Taking a deep drink from his bottled water, he thanked the young woman and headed back out into the sun and salt water.

www.ingramcontent.com/pod-product-compliance
Lightning Source LLC
Chambersburg PA
CBHW052022020726

47501CB00004B/1195